D0998184

FREDDY

and the

SPACE SHIP

WALTER R. BROOKS

Illustrated by Kurt Wiese

THE OVERLOOK PRESS

NEW YORK

FREDDY

and the

SPACE SHIP

If you enjoyed this book, very likely you will be interested not only in the other Freddy books published in this series, but also in joining the *Friends of Freddy*, an organization of Freddy devotees.

We will be pleased to hear from any reader about our "Freddy" publishing program. You can easily contact us by logging on to either THE OVERLOOK PRESS website or the Freddy website.

The website addresses are as follows:

THE OVERLOOK PRESS
www.overlookpress.com

FREDDY
www.friendsoffreddy.org

We look forward to hearing from you soon.

This edition first published in paperback in the United States in 2011 by

The Overlook Press, Peter Mayer Publishers, Inc.
141 Wooster Street
New York, NY 10012
www.overlookpress.com
For bulk orders and special sales, please contact sales@overlookny.com

Library of Congress Cataloging-in-Publication Data

Brooks, Walter R., 1886-1958.
Freddy and the space ship / Walter R. Brooks ; illustrated by Kurt Wiese.
p. cm.
Summary: Freddy the pig and some barnyard friends take off for Mars in Mr. Bean's space ship, but things go awry when Mrs. Peppercorn fiddles with the controls and they wind up in a stranger place than they ever imagined.
[1. Pigs—Fiction. 2. Domestic animals—Fiction. 3. Space flight—Interplanetary voyages—Fiction.] I. Wiese, Kurt, 1887-1974, ill. II. Title.
PZ7.B7994 Frag 2001 [Fic]—DC21 00-050150

Manufactured in the United States of America
ISBN 978-1-59020-469-6
2 4 6 8 10 9 7 5 3 1

FREDDY

and the

SPACE SHIP

CHAPTER

1

Mrs. Bean turned another page in the photograph album. "This," she said, "is Uncle Ben when he was eight years old."

She was sitting in the rocking chair on the

back porch. Jinx, the cat, was perched on the arm of the chair, and Freddy, the pig, was sitting beside it, where he could see the pictures.

"My goodness," said Freddy, "he certainly doesn't look as if he'd be smart enough to build space ships and things."

"I could wish he wasn't so smart," Mrs. Bean said. "That great rocket contraption he's been working on for the last six months in the upper pasture—probably blow us all to glory when he sets it off." She looked up and across the barnyard and the nearer fields to where the tall spire of the giant rocket stood out against the sky. Then she turned another page in the album. "This is Mr. Bean when he was three."

The picture showed a chubby little boy in a plaid dress. He had a frightened look, and his hair was cut in a sort of bang low on his forehead.

"Golly!" said Jinx. "Isn't it funny to see Mr. Bean without his whiskers!"

"Well, at three years old, what do you expect?" said Freddy.

"I don't know. I guess I thought he was born with them," the cat said. "I can't imagine seeing any expression on Mr. Bean's face, but he really has one in that picture."

Mrs. Bean chuckled. "He had those whiskers when we were married," she said, "so I've never seen any expression on his face either." She turned a page. "This is Cousin Matilda Cassowary. She's not really my cousin; she's a second cousin twice removed of Mr. Bean's Aunt Jennie's first husband's sister. Not very closely related, but I always think of her as a member of the family, I guess because she sends me a Christmas card every year." She lifted her head and sniffed the air. "I smell smoke."

"It's those people who moved into the Grimby house, up in the Big Woods, last fall—they're burning brush," Freddy said.

It was a clear day. Up beyond the tall finger of the rocket ship, they could see the dark line of the Bean woods, edging the upper pasture. These woods went on to a back road, and beyond the back road the Big Woods began. A thin bluish haze of smoke hung above them.

"I hope they'll be careful," Mrs. Bean said. "The woods are pretty dry; 'twouldn't take much to get 'em blazing."

"I don't like those people," said Jinx. "When they first moved in I went up to call—"

"Went up to inspect their garbage pail, most likely," Freddy put in.

"Nothing of the kind!" Jinx snapped. "When a new family moves into the neighborhood, it's the polite thing to go call on 'em. Us cats are pretty particular about things like that. Of course if a saucer of milk is put out—well, it wouldn't be good manners to just leave it standing there."

"Oh, sure," Freddy said. "Even if they threw you out an old fish head, you'd smack your lips over it, just to show how you appreciated their kind thought."

"A fish head ain't a kind thought; it's an insult," said the cat. "But look, do you want to hear about this or don't you?"

"I've heard it forty times," said Freddy, "but maybe Mrs. Bean hasn't, so go ahead."

"Well," said Jinx, "there was me, strolling up the path to the front porch, all licked and polished up for my call, and full of good will; and then—my gosh!—out came that Mrs. Bismuth and chased me off into the bushes with a nasty old wet mop! And I ask you—is that any way to

Around him as he ran galloped the other farm animals.

treat a caller? Not in my etiquette book it isn't."

"Depends on the caller," Freddy said. "Some folks think cats just smooch up to you to see what they can get out of you. They—" He broke off. "Hey!" he said. "Look at that smoke now!"

The thin blue haze in the north had given place to billowing black smoke clouds, and as they stared, a long tongue of flame licked up towards the sky, and another, and then another.

Mr. Bean came running out of the barn. "Mrs. B.," he called, "call up the Centerboro fire house. Those consarned Bismuths have set the Big Woods on fire!" He grabbed a shovel and dashed off up the slope towards the woods.

Around him as he ran galloped the other farm animals: Hank, the old white horse, the three cows, Mrs. Wiggins, Mrs. Wurzburger and Mrs. Wogus, Robert and Georgie, the dogs, and Bill, the goat, with the smaller animals trailing along behind. Freddy and Jinx followed.

The Big Woods were really blazing now. Above the treetops flames fifty feet high roared and crackled. The animals set to work to help Mr. Bean dig a trench across the line of fire to protect the home woods. Pretty soon the Centerboro Fire Department arrived in its bright red trucks, and long hose lines sucked up water from the duck pond and poured it into the fire. Other helpers came, by twos and threes, carrying spades and hose and axes, and soon they had surrounded the fire and cleared inflammable stuff from its path so that it could no longer spread.

It was nearly dark before the fire was at last under control. More than half of the Big Woods had been burned. The Grimby house was of course nothing but a smoking ruin, and when the animals at last came back down to the barnyard, grimy with soot and ashes, they found the Bismuth family, surrounded by what few things they had been able to save from the fire, sitting on the back porch of the farmhouse. Mrs. Bismuth was a weak, whiny sort of woman, and she was crying, and the two children, Carl and Bella, were sitting one on each side of her and looking miserable, and Mr. Bismuth, who was a tall thin man with small eyes set close to a long sharp nose that was twisted to the left, was talking. All four were eating cookies and drinking milk faster than Freddy had ever seen anybody eat before. And Mr. Bismuth, though he was talking all the time, was eating faster than all the other three put together.

"Nothing to worry about," he was saying. "Nothing at all! Ha, ha; I should say not! Oh sure, burned up the house, burned up the furniture—but it didn't burn up the Bismuths. Buy another house, buy more furniture—ha ha!— Bismuth's in business again!"

Mr. Bismuth's little laugh seemed to irritate Mr. Bean. "Maybe it's ha, ha, and maybe it ain't," he remarked. "What you going to use for money?"

Mr. Bismuth crammed two more molasses cookies into his mouth. "A Bismuth never worries about money. Ha, ha, I guess not! You can't keep a Bismuth down. Any more cookies in the house?" he asked, peering into the now empty crock. "Real good cookies, they are, but not very filling."

"They filled that crock when it was brought out here," Mr. Bean said drily, but Mrs. Bean said: "Tut, tut, Mr. B., mind your manners!" For she wasn't merely sorry for the Bismuths because they had lost everything they possessed in the fire. She felt responsible for them. It was she who had got them to come live in the

Grimby house in the first place. For she and Mrs. Bismuth were cousins; they had been brought up together; but when Mrs. Bismuth had married and moved to Cleveland they hadn't seen much of each other. It was only last fall that, having learned that Mr. Bismuth had been out of work for months, she had written suggesting that Mrs. Bismuth and the children come stay in the Grimby house until Mr. Bismuth could get on his feet again.

So the Bismuths came. The Beans were surprised that Mr. Bismuth came too; they had expected that he would stay in Cleveland and look for a job. But he said it was just as easy to look for a job in Centerboro, and indeed at first he did look, and with Mr. Bean's help he worked on the Grimby house to make it livable. But he didn't get a job. There always seemed to be something he didn't like about those that were offered him. "But Ed'll get a job; don't you worry," Mrs. Bismuth said.

Mrs. Bean said she certainly hoped so.

Then came the fire. And when the Bismuths came wandering down from the woods, grimy with smoke and looking very woe-begone indeed, she had of course told them that they must

come and stay at the farm until they could find
another house to move into.

So when the cookies were gone, Mrs. Bean
went into the kitchen and made up a big platter
of ham sandwiches and brought them out, and
the Bismuths ate them all up in three minutes.

Well that was just the beginning. The Bismuths settled down on the Bean farm like a
flock of grasshoppers, and they ate and ate and
ate. They ate three big meals a day and they also
ate before breakfast and before dinner and all
afternoon and they took stuff to bed with them
and ate it before they went to sleep. At the table
there was such a flickering of knives and forks
and such a chomping of jaws that the Beans got
up almost as hungry as when they had sat down.
Mr. Bean would reach out with his fork to take
another chop, and two or three Bismuth forks
would dart in under his and spear the last ones,
leaving for him nothing but a little spot of
grease on the platter. Mr. Bean didn't like this
much, but there wasn't anything he could do
about it, because, as Mrs. Bean said, after all
they had invited the Bismuths to stay.

"Until they find a new place to live," she said,
"we'll just have to put up with them. And Mrs.

Bismuth does try to help with the housework."

"Help!" Mr. Bean exclaimed disgustedly. "Try to pick up a fork that woman has washed and it's so sticky you have to pry it off the tablecloth. Give her an egg to fry and it's so tough you could use it to nail over a mouse hole. I don't know how she does it. And that Ed Bismuth! Been down helping Uncle Ben work on his space ship. I never saw a man could do so much damage just with a little pair of pliers. Knocked three holes in the side of the ship, broke the pliers, and hit Ben in the eye with his elbow—all just tightening one little nut on the instrument panel. I bet if he tries to fix that broken windowpane for you he'll tear out the side of the house."

"Oh well, it won't be long," said Mrs. Bean. "Poor things, we can't just put them out when they have no place to go."

But before long it was pretty clear that the Bismuths had no intention of trying to find another house to move into. They read the "Houses to Let" ads in the Centerboro *Guardian,* and then Mr. Bismuth would go into town and look at the houses. But when he got back it was always the same story: something the matter with the house. Either the roof leaked or the furnace didn't work or the stairs were shaky. One place he turned down because he said there were mice.

"I'm deathly afraid of mice!" said Mrs. Bismuth. "Deathly!" And she began to cry.

"Mice!" said Mr. Bean. "There's mice in this house." And he gave a little whistle and the four Bean mice—Eek and Quik and Eeny and Cousin Augustus—trooped out from under the stove and stood at attention.

But if he had hoped to scare Mrs. Bismuth into leaving, he failed. She sat up and wiped away her tears quickly and said: "My, my! Aren't they cute!"

"Thought you was afraid of mice, ma'am," said Mr. Bean.

"Oh, not mice like *these!*" Mr. Bismuth said quickly. "It's those big mice with the long teeth and the blue spots all over 'em—that Centerboro house was swarmin' with 'em. 'Fraid of them myself. Yes sir, a Bismuth ain't afraid of much, but those big blue-spotted mice—oh boy! Big as lions, some of 'em. Ha, ha! Small lions, of course."

The mice went back under the stove and had

a conference, and later told Freddy. "How'd it be," they said, "if we dressed some of the rabbits up as mice—pinned long tails on 'em and painted blue spots on 'em—and then—"

"No," said Freddy. "Don't you see?—that's just a story Mr. Bismuth made up. If the Beans had lions and tigers in the cellar, the Bismuths would stay just the same. They aren't afraid of anything except having to pay for their meals."

In the meantime Uncle Ben was putting the finishing touches on the Benjamin Bean Space Ship. He had done all the work himself, having made enough from the sale of the Benjamin Bean Improved Self-Filling Piggy Bank—the story of which is told elsewhere—to pay for all his materials. The day before the fire he had taken the smaller animals through the ship and shown them the control room in the nose, the living quarters on the level below, and the storage space for fuel on the lower level. He had explained how the ship worked, but it is doubtful if any of the animals understood the explanation, for Uncle Ben was not a talkative man. It is all very well to explain things in words of one syllable, but to explain them in sentences of one syllable is not very easy. Indeed sometimes Un-

cle Ben didn't even use one complete syllable—
he just grunted.

Of course Freddy was able to help Uncle Ben
out in his explanations, for he had read a lot of
books about space travel, and so understood
how the ship could be fired like a rocket up
through the earth's atmosphere, and could
cruise along through empty space until it came
close to the planet at which it was aimed. Then
he knew that the tremendous speed had to be
cut down so that the ship wouldn't be smashed
when it landed. This would be done by turning
the ship around so that the rocket could be fired
again at the planet, acting as a brake as they
approached.

After the animals had been shown through
the ship, Uncle Ben said: "Mars, next stop.
Who wants to go?"

Of course they all wanted to go. "I want to
go!" "Take me!" "Please take me!" they yelled,
and they crowded around him and jumped up
and down until at last he held up his hand.
"Four animals," he said. "You." He pointed at
Freddy. "You," at Jinx. "You and you," at
Charles, the rooster, and Georgie, the little
brown dog. He took out a notebook and wrote

down some figures in it, looked at them a minute, then snapped the book shut. "Week from Friday, eight twenty-one A.M. sharp. You four be here." Then he turned and climbed back into the ship and shut the door.

There was no arguing with one of Uncle Ben's decisions. The animals who had not been chosen wandered dejectedly away, but the four who were to go went down to the pig pen to decide what they had better take along.

CHAPTER

2

A day or two after the fire, Freddy was sitting in his study in the pig pen, writing a short fare-well poem which he intended to recite to the assembled animals just before taking off for Mars.

Farewell my friends, farewell my foes;
To distant planets Freddy goes;
To face grave perils he intends.
Farewell my foes, goodbye my friends.

He had written this much when there was a tap on the door.

When interrupted in the middle of a poetic composition, Freddy sometimes found it difficult to speak in plain prose. So instead of just saying: "Come in," he said:

"Turn the knob and open the door.
What on earth are you waiting for?"

But the door didn't open. Instead, the tapping went on.

Freddy said irritably: "Open the door! Take just one more step
And come inside off my front doorstep."

And then as the tapping continued— "Oh, gosh," he said (in prose) and got up and threw the door open. A very plump and pompous middle-aged duck waddled importantly in.

"Oh, it's you, Wes," said Freddy. "Sorry; I didn't realize you couldn't reach the knob. What's poisoning your mind this morning?"

Uncle Wesley lived up by the duck pond with

his two nieces, Alice and Emma. He was rather tiresome, even for a duck, but Alice and Emma were so fond of him that the farm animals put up with his nonsense.

"I wish to put a letter in the next number of the Bean Home News," said Uncle Wesley. This was the weekly newspaper which Freddy published for the animals on the farm. He handed Freddy a rumpled brown paper bag on which the letter had been written with a very hard pencil.

Freddy took it over close to the window and squinted at it. This was really not much help, for the window was so dirty that, as Jinx had once remarked, it was really harder to see anything there than it was in the darkest corners of the room.

"H'm, let's see," said Freddy, and started reading the letter. " 'A crocodile exists up at the duck pond which I wish to sing to this afternoon—' What on earth, Wes!"

"It's not 'sing,' it's 'bring,' " said Uncle Wesley testily. "And the word isn't 'crocodile,' it's 'condition.' Can't you read plain English? 'A condition exists up at the duck pond which I wish to bring to your attention.' "

Freddy said: "Oh. Sounds much more interesting the way I read it. But perhaps you'd better read it to me. Because I see something down here that seems to say that 'we have five heavy hippos in the pond.' Good gracious, Wes; hippos in addition to all your crocodile trouble—?"

"Oh, don't be so witty," said the duck angrily. "It's 'happy,' not 'hippos.' It says: 'we have been very happy in the pond.' If you're not going to pay any attention—"

"All right, all right; you read it," Freddy said.

So Uncle Wesley read the letter. It stated that when the Centerboro firemen had pumped water from the duck pond to put out the fire, they had so stirred it up that a good deal of the muddy bottom had been pumped out too. And to ducks, the mud in the bottom of a pond is just the same as a refrigerator—when they get hungry they dive and hunt around in the mud for their dinners. It doesn't seem very appetizing, but ducks like it.

Freddy didn't see what could be done about putting the mud back, but he said he'd print the letter, and he was trying to get off the subject of mud by inquiring about the health of Alice and Emma, when he happened to glance out of the window and saw several figures moving up along the edge of the upper pasture towards the Benjamin Bean space ship.

Everything Freddy saw through the small wavy windowpanes was always so twisted out of shape that he couldn't tell what it was. And the dirt made it even harder. Freddy liked it that way; he said that things were twice as interesting seen through those panes. It is not specially exciting to see a cow going by, but when you look out and see a two-headed giant anteater, it gives you something to wonder about. That's the way Freddy felt about it. Jinx, a frequent caller, didn't agree. He said that the sight of a lot of misshapen prehistoric monsters prowling around outside gave him cold chills. But cats don't get as much fun out of imagining things as other animals do.

So for a second or two Freddy amused himself by watching what appeared to be a procession of giants, some with very short legs, others with heads as long and narrow as cucumbers, marching past. But when these were followed by a group of dwarfs, one with six legs, he got up and went to the door. For whether giants or dwarfs or just ordinary people, there were too

"Why it wouldn't hold more than two people."

many of them. They must be strangers, and what were so many strangers doing up here at the farm?

Uncle Wesley followed Freddy outside. "Well, upon my soul!" he exclaimed. "Who are these persons?" For straggling up towards the space ship from cars which they had parked in the road outside the gate were perhaps twenty people, and as they watched, two more cars drew up.

"We'd better find out," said Freddy. "My goodness, there's old Mrs. Peppercorn from Centerboro! What on earth—?" He went down to meet a little old lady in an old fashioned bonnet who was stumping up the slope with the help of a large umbrella. "How do you do, Mrs. Peppercorn? What has brought you way up here so far from home?"

"Judge Willey brought me," she said, "if it's any business of yours, young man." She peered at Freddy. "Seems as if I'd seen you somewhere before," she said.

"Why, I'm Freddy," said the pig. "You know me."

She peered closer. "Well, so I do, so I do," she said. "Thought you were that fat Scripture boy

—you're enough like him to be his brother. Well, Freddy, are you going too?"

"Good morning, Frederick; good morning," said Judge Willey, coming up. "You are also, I presume, a member of our little band of adventurers?"

"Say, what *is* this?" Freddy asked. "Going where? What adventure?"

"Why to Mars of course," said the Judge, and Mrs. Peppercorn said: "I supposed you'd be the first one aboard the ship."

"Aboard!" Freddy exclaimed. "Goodness, you don't mean that all these people think they can go in the space ship? Why it wouldn't hold more than two people."

"What's this?" demanded the Judge. "You say there's no room?" And Mrs. Peppercorn said: "Nonsense! We've paid our fare. Of course we're going."

"Look," said Freddy; "I don't understand this at all. Uncle Ben's going to try to get to Mars, but the only ones who are going with him are Jinx and Charles and me. There's no room in the nose of the rocket for anyone else."

Judge Willey looked perplexed, but Mrs. Peppercorn pounded her umbrella on the ground. "I'm a'goin', and that's flat," she said. "I've paid five dollars for my ticket, and I'm a'goin', and I'd like to see anybody try to stop me!" And she started on.

"I don't get this ticket business," Freddy said. "You say you bought tickets?"

"We did; we bought them from the duly appointed representative of the Benjamin Bean Spaceship Co. Tall thin man with a long crooked nose."

"Mr. Bismuth!" Freddy exclaimed. "Why, he has no right to sell tickets! Golly, we'd better get Bismuth and straighten this out." He turned to Uncle Wesley. "Wes," he said, "will you go tell Uncle Ben about this? I'll try to find Bismuth. I guess he'll have some explaining to do."

Mr. Bismuth wasn't around anywhere, so Freddy and the Judge hurried up to where an angry crowd surrounded the space ship. In the doorway at the top of the little ladder stood Uncle Ben, and at the foot of the ladder was Mrs. Peppercorn. She was addressing the crowd. "Are we a'goin' to be put off with soft words and excuses?" she demanded.

"No!" yelled the crowd, among whom

Freddy recognized most of the solid business-
men of Centerboro. Evidently Mr. Bismuth had
gone right up one side of Main Street and down
the other, selling his tickets. At five dollars a
head he must have taken in well over a hundred
dollars. Freddy wondered if they'd ever see him
again.

Mrs. Peppercorn turned and shook her umbrella at Uncle Ben. "Now, Mr. Benjamin
Bean," she said, "are you going to let us aboard
that there ship, or are we coming aboard anyway?"

Uncle Ben was on a spot. He was a fine me-
chanic but no talker. To make a speech and explain something to a crowd was impossible for
him. He stood there looking sort of hopeless,
and then he caught sight of Freddy and beck-
oned to him. So Freddy ducked around Mrs.
Peppercorn and climbed halfway up the ladder,
then turned.

"Ladies and gentlemen!" he shouted. "You
have been deceived and cheated. But not, *not*
by Uncle Ben! Listen to me!"

Freddy was well known and highly respected
in Centerboro. Those who had never required
his services as a detective admired him as a poet,

and those who cared nothing for poetry respected his standing as President of the First Animal Bank. So they listened while he explained what had happened.

But they were far from satisfied with an explanation. "We want our money back!" they shouted. "This Bismuth man—he lives with you; you're responsible for him. It's up to you to bring him out here and make him give back our money."

Freddy started to say that he'd try to find Mr. Bismuth, but Mrs. Peppercorn was getting impatient. "I don't want my money back!" she said, "and what's more, I won't take it back. I'm a'goin' to Mars!" She swung her umbrella over her head like a sword and charged up the ladder. Freddy ducked away from the swipe she made at him, and she climbed nimbly past him, pushed Uncle Ben aside, and went into the ship.

The crowd milled around and seemed undecided whether to try to follow Mrs. Peppercorn, or to continue demanding their money. But Freddy had spoken a word to Judge Willey, who now stepped forward.

"My friends," he said, "you have been grossly

deceived. The man who sold us these tickets is a certain Bismuth, a fraud and very evidently a crook. Mr. Benjamin Bean has no intention of taking passengers to Mars, for the very good reason that there is no room in the ship for passengers. This Bismuth has taken our money and run off with it. My friend, Freddy, tells me that, as a partner in the well known detective agency of Frederick and Wiggins, he will at once put every operative in his employ at work tracking down the said Bismuth. He assures me that full restitution will be made to each and every one of us.

"Now most of us know Mr. Benjamin; we know his reputation for probity and fair dealing. We also know Freddy—so well that I believe it unnecessary to remind you of his skill in detective work, in tracking down criminals, in clearing the innocent from false charges and in soaking the guilty with everything in the book. I believe that we can safely leave this affair in the capable hands—or should I say trotters?—of our respected friend."

There was some applause at this and Freddy took a bow; then the crowd slowly straggled back to the parked cars.

Freddy went on up the ladder and into the ship. He climbed up through the hatchway from the living quarters into the control room. As his head came above the floor level, he saw Uncle Ben backed against the wall with his hands over his head, and the point of Mrs. Peppercorn's umbrella poised ready to jab him in the stomach. With one hand the old lady held the umbrella drawn back like a bayonet; the other was on the big valve which controlled the fuel for the rocket.

"I've a good mind to give it a twist and see what happens," she was saying, and her hand tightened on the valve. She caught sight of Freddy. "Keep off, young pig, or I'll do it anyway."

"No, no!" Uncle Ben begged her. "Dangerous. Ship's not ready."

Freddy knew that if she turned that valve it would fire the rocket, and the ship would whiz off up into the sky. It would travel up through the earth's atmosphere, and off into space; and since it would be fired more than a week earlier than Uncle Ben had planned, it probably wouldn't come anywhere near Mars, but would go circling around the earth like a very small

moon for the next million years. The idea of
spending even a hundred years whirling around
the sky with Mrs. Peppercorn and Uncle Ben
didn't appeal to him much. But before he could
think of anything to do Mrs. Peppercorn said:

"Well, make up your mind. Do I give it a
twist or don't I?"

Uncle Ben sighed. "I give in," he said. "You
can go." And Mrs. Peppercorn took her hand
off the valve and dropped the point of the umbrella.

"What goes on here?" Freddy asked. "You
don't mean you're letting her go with us to
Mars?"

"Got to," Uncle Ben said. He looked hope-
lessly at Freddy.

"Well," said the pig, "I suppose you couldn't
help it." He looked thoughtfully at the old lady.
"Of course I suppose she understands the dan-
gers of the trip. You've probably told her what
the Martians are like, and shown her pictures
of them."

"Pictures?" said Uncle Ben. "Aren't any pictures."

Freddy winked at him. "Guess you've forgotten. I mean those pictures Professor Gasswitz

sent you—sort of like big two-legged spiders they are, with great yellow eyes and long poison fangs."

But Mrs. Peppercorn wasn't impressed. "Must be pretty," she said drily. "I'd enjoy a chat with one of 'em."

Freddy gave up. "O K, so you're going," he said. "Well, Uncle Ben, you'd better explain to her how the ship works. I'll go try to find Mr. Bismuth."

CHAPTER

3

Mrs. Bismuth didn't seem much worried about the disappearance of her husband. When Freddy told her what had happened, and that Mr. Bismuth had apparently run off with all the money he had collected, she did indeed burst into tears. But when Freddy tried to comfort her, and assured her that they would find Mr. Bismuth and make him give back the money, she explained (between sobs) that she had no fear that he was a thief: she wept, she stated, because of Freddy's lack of confidence in her noble husband.

"Oh, how can you say such things about Pa?" she wailed. "Pa is a gentleman; Pa would not steal. Children, close your ears; do not listen to such dreadful stories about your noble Pa." She wept bitterly, and the two little Bismuths wept with her.

But Freddy said: "Your noble Pa had better come back with the money he took for those tickets or our noble sheriff will put him in jail."

Uncle Ben felt pretty badly about it. He said he was going down to Centerboro and pay five dollars back to everybody who had bought a ticket from Mr. Bismuth. But when he came to count up his money he had only eight dollars. He had spent all the rest for materials to build the space ship.

So Mr. Bean said he'd advance the money. "These Bismuths," he said; "they're relatives, ain't they? Well, then, we're responsible for them."

Freddy said: "I don't see why either you or Uncle Ben should have to give back the money just because the one that stole it married Mrs. Bean's cousin." He even argued with Mr. Bean about it, which is something almost none of the animals ever did. But finally Mrs. Bean said: "You can argue till you're blue in the face, Freddy, but if Mr. Bean feels that we're responsible, then we're responsible. You're right, Mr. B., as always."

That settled it, and Mr. Bean was just getting ready to hitch Hank up to the phaeton and drive down to Centerboro to get the money from the bank, when Mr. Bismuth himself came riding up the road on a brand new bicycle.

Mrs. Bismuth was pretty emotional; that is to say, she yelled a lot when it wasn't really necessary. She gave a loud yell now and started to fall over in a faint, and Mr. Bismuth jumped off his bicycle and propped her up, and the two little Bismuths, who were also emotional, began to cry again—probably from joy, this time.

Mrs. Bismuth's yell had brought the Beans

and all the animals out into the barnyard, and they surrounded Mr. Bismuth in an angry group, demanding to know where the money was that he had collected for tickets. But Mr. Bismuth held up his hands and said laughingly: "Please! Please! Why, my friends, here's a great fuss over nothing at all. It was just a joke—ha, ha!—a Bismuth must have his little joke, mustn't he? They'll all get their money back. I'm off for Centerboro now to give it to 'em."

Mr. Bean looked hard at him. "See that you do," he said. "We don't care for that kind of joke on this farm. Come along, Uncle Ben." And the Beans went into the house.

But Freddy wasn't satisfied. "Wait a minute," he said as the other animals began to straggle away. "I want to know where that bicycle came from. You didn't have it when you left here, Mr. Bismuth."

"Well now, ain't you the sharp-eyed one!" said Mr. Bismuth admiringly. "Who'd ha' thought you'd noticed that! No sir, I didn't, and that's a fact. But I'll tell you about it. Ha, ha! A Bismuth don't have any secrets from his friends. Bein' a plumber by trade, I done a

The phaeton went into the ditch.

little plumbing job for Dr. Wintersip. When I was finished, he says: 'How you gettin' back to the farm?' 'Walk,' I says, and he says: 'All that ways? Why that's terrible! Here,' he says, 'take this here bicycle—I don't hardly ever use it.' 'Oh, no,' I says; 'a Bismuth don't ever take more'n what he's entitled to, and you already paid me well for the job.' But he insisted, and—well, I took it. Real nice of him, eh?''

Freddy didn't say anything, and after a minute Mr. Bismuth untied a bag from the handlebars and gave it to his wife. "Some candy and little cakes for you and the kids," he said. "I'll probably be back to supper—hungry as a hunter, too, likely. So tell Mrs. Bean to save me plenty." He jumped on the bicycle and rode out of the gate.

Mrs. Bismuth and the children opened the bag and began gobbling the candy and cakes as fast as they could. They didn't offer the animals any. Freddy thought there must be several dollars' worth of stuff in the bag, and he wondered if some of the ticket money hadn't bought it, for he was sure the Bismuths couldn't have that much to spend on candy. He went into the barn where Mr. Bean was starting to unhitch Hank from the phaeton. "Would you let me drive into Centerboro?" he said. "I'd like to check Mr. Bismuth's story. I don't think he was telling the truth."

"Know durn well he wasn't," said Mr. Bean. "Go ahead. But no racing." Mr. Bean was referring to the last time Freddy had driven Hank to town, when he had raced a trailer truck and had been sideswiped.

It had been more Hank's fault than Freddy's, as a matter of fact. Going up a long hill the truck had slowed down, and Hank had tried to pass. But the truck wouldn't let them by, and the driver leaned out and jeered at them, calling Hank "king of the boneyard," and "old snort-and-heave." This made Hank mad. He took the bit in his teeth and tried to pass anyway.

Freddy protested, but he couldn't pull on the reins to stop Hank, because there weren't any. Mr. Bean never used reins to steer the horse with; he just told Hank where he wanted to go, and Hank took him there. It was a handy arrangement, but in this case it didn't work well. The phaeton went into the ditch, a wheel came off, and Freddy was thrown out and hit his nose on a rock. Although the phaeton really belonged to the animals, who had brought it back from their trip to Florida, Mr. Bean was upset because he said both of them might have been killed.

Hank was more careful this time and they got into Centerboro all right and drew up in front of Dr. Wintersip's little white house. Freddy jumped out and ran up the steps and gave a pull at the old-fashioned doorbell. But instead of ringing a bell, the knob came right out in his hand and he nearly fell backwards off the porch. He started to knock, but just then the door opened and Dr. Wintersip stuck his head out.

"Well, well," he said. "It's Freddy. Thought I heard someone. Come in." Then he saw that Freddy was still holding the bell knob. "Aha," he said, "I expected that. That bell was one of the things your Mr. Bismuth repaired for me."

"I thought he said he did a plumbing job for you," Freddy said.

"He did several jobs. If he'd stayed a little longer I guess I'd have had to move out of the house. Come in; I'll show you."

They went out into the kitchen. There were

muddy tracks all over the floor, and beside the sink was a big hole in the wall, with a heap of plaster under it. There was also a good deal of water on the floor.

"This Bismuth person answered an ad I had in the paper for a handyman to come make a few repairs," Dr. Wintersip said. "He gave Mr. Bean as a reference, so I thought he must be all right. First thing he fixed was the back door. It would blow open in the wind because the latch was loose. 'Ha, ha,' says Bismuth: 'we'll fix that all right!' And he did. He took half a dozen spikes and nailed it shut. Now we can't use that door any more.

"Well, I thought maybe he'd misunderstood me, so I had him fix the doorbell, and a couple of other little things, and then there was a little leak in the hot water faucet out here. He looked at it and said: 'You got any adhesive plaster?' I thought maybe he'd cut himself, so I got him some. He tried to mend the leak with it, and of course when we turned the water on again it blew out all over everything. Then—well, I don't know what he did, but you see what a mess he made. And the water won't run at all out here now."

Freddy said: "Dear, dear!" and he said: "Tut, tut!" and he said: "Mr. Bean will be pretty upset about this. I'm sure that he'll make things right. By the way, Mr. Bismuth came home with a bicycle he said you'd given him. You didn't, did you?"

"A bicycle?" said Dr. Wintersip. "No, of course not. I . . ." He stopped suddenly. "Gracious me, you don't suppose . . . I left my bicycle out back . . ." He made for the back door, but of course that was spiked shut. They had to go out the front door and around to the back porch. The bicycle wasn't there.

Freddy had about used up all his apologies. He just stood and looked at Dr. Wintersip and Dr. Wintersip looked at him and they both groaned. Then Freddy said: "I'll get it back for you," and he turned to go down off the porch. But as he stepped to the edge, the board he stepped on was one that Mr. Bismuth had repaired the floor with and forgotten to nail down. So it tipped up behind Freddy and smacked him in the rear, and he fell off the porch into a rain barrel about half full of rain water.

Freddy went into the barrel headfirst, but he

didn't go all the way in because he was too plump. He just went in up to his shoulders. Dr. Wintersip caught him by the legs and pulled him out, and Freddy wiped the water, and a few dead leaves that had been in it, off his face and said very coldly and quietly: "Thank you." And then he left. But Dr. Wintersip sat down on the porch and put his head in his hands and moaned.

CHAPTER

4

Hank hadn't seen Freddy fall into the barrel, but when he heard about it he thought it was pretty funny. As they drove back up Main Street he laughed so hard that people turned and looked after him, and then they began laughing too. They didn't know the joke, but they had probably heard the saying: "It's enough to make a horse laugh," and so they laughed anyway because if it made Hank laugh, they thought it must be a really good one.

Hank didn't stop until Freddy threatened him with the whip, and then he sobered down. But he kept making remarks. He said that he'd always heard that rainwater was good for the complexion, and then he would keep turning around and looking back at Freddy and admiring him. "Lovely!" he said. "Lovely! The skin you love to touch. Like rose petals, really." "Blooming!" he said. "Positively blooming!"

Freddy stood it for about so long and then he thought he'd get out and walk, and he was just doing so when he caught sight of Mr. Bismuth in front of Beller & Rohr's, talking to Judge Willey. The bicycle was propped against a post.

Freddy went up to him but before he could say anything, Mr. Bismuth said: "Aha, the great detective! Sniffing along the trail, I presume, of some arch-criminal? Ha, ha! Not mine, I hope."

Freddy said: "Yes, yours. I want you to take Dr. Wintersip's bicycle back to him."

"What? This bicycle?" Mr. Bismuth demanded. "My dear boy, the good doctor *gave* it to me! He *gave* me this—"

Freddy interrupted. "He didn't do anything of the kind. If he doesn't get it back he's going to have you arrested."

"Arrested?" Mr. Bismuth started back dramatically. "Arrest a Bismuth? Ha, ha, my boy, you are joking."

"I'm not joking!" said Freddy. "I have just been to see Dr. Wintersip."

"I see, I see," said Mr. Bismuth striking his forehead. "The good doctor has changed his mind. He regrets having given me the bicycle. Now who would have thought that that kindly man would turn out to be an Indian giver! Well I shall return it." He reached for the bicycle, but Judge Willey said:

"Just a moment. You were about to return to me the five dollars which I paid you for a ticket to Mars."

"Don't be alarmed." Mr. Bismuth leaned the bicycle against himself and reached for his pocket. "You shall have it, sir. A Bismuth never forgets." He turned to Freddy. "All a joke, you know, really—this selling tickets. As if you could buy a ticket to Mars for five dollars, when it

The horse seized him by the collar and lifted him clear of the ground.

costs two just to go to Syracuse on the bus! Ha, ha! It always amuses a Bismuth to fool people. All kindly meant, of course. I am returning all the money today, with a little gift, so that there will be no hard feelings. I—" His hand had been sliding into his pocket and now it stopped and a look of consternation came over his face. The hand came out empty, and he held it up and stared at it. "Nothing!" he shouted. "The money is gone! I have been robbed!" He dropped the bicycle and began feeling himself all over, patting his pockets and fumbling inside his coat. "Robbed!" he cried. "Ha! They can't do this to me—the villains!" He looked wildly around. "Where's the sheriff?" he demanded. "Where's an officer of the law?"

Freddy didn't believe for a minute that Mr. Bismuth had been robbed. He remembered the big bag of candy, and he was sure that what was left of the ticket money was still in one of those pockets. That inside breast pocket in the coat bulged suspiciously. He went over and spoke a word in a low voice to Hank, who was standing by the curb, and the horse moved up behind Mr. Bismuth, seized him by the collar in his strong teeth and lifted him clear of the ground. Then Freddy said politely: "Let me help you," and before Mr. Bismuth, who was struggling uselessly, could stop him, he reached into the inside pocket and drew out a wad of bills.

Mr. Bismuth stopped struggling. "Let me down, please," he said with dignity, and when he had pulled his coat down from around his ears, he held out his hand for the money. "How in the world did it get into *that* pocket?" he said. "I felt there, too. You both saw me. Well, I'm certainly glad it was not stolen. Just hand it over, Freddy, and I'll—"

"You'll run off with it again, I suppose," Freddy said. "Thanks, I guess I'd better take care of it. Judge Willey, here's your five. And now we'll go in and give Mr. Rohr his."

Mr. Bismuth protested. "I'm the one that should give it back," he said. "You're just spoiling the joke and making it look as if I was trying to cheat these people."

"That's right," said Freddy. "Come on—or do you want Hank to help you?"

Mr. Bismuth didn't. So he followed along as Freddy went up Main Street, stopping in the stores and paying back the people who had

given up five dollars for a ticket. Mr. Bismuth
made a little explanation each time, how it had
all been done in a spirit of good clean fun, and
of course he intended to give the money back
all the time, and he hoped there were no hard
feelings.

Word had got around that he was paying
back the money, and before they'd gone far the
ticket buyers came pouring out of the stores and
surrounded them. Freddy paid them off as
quickly as possible, but pretty soon the money
was gone and there were still seven who hadn't
been paid. That meant that Mr. Bismuth had
already spent thirty-five dollars of the money
he had taken in, but of course he wouldn't admit it, and he said that those seven people had
never bought tickets from him. They got pretty
mad. Freddy promised them that he would see
to it that they got their money back, but a Mr.
Gridley, the school principal, hit Mr. Bismuth
on the nose, bending it still farther to the left,
and there would have been a free for all fight
if Hank hadn't got Mr. Bismuth by the collar
and dragged him away. Freddy left the bicycle
with Mr. Rohr, who promised to phone Dr.
Wintersip about it, and then he got Mr. Bis-

muth into the phaeton and they went back to the farm.

Mr. Bismuth tied his nose up in a handkerchief, and when they got home and his wife and children saw him there was such a howling and sobbing that there was no chance for Mr. Bean to get any explanation out of him. Mrs. Bean got a hot water bag and Mrs. Bismuth tried to tie it on his nose, and the little Bismuths climbed around on him and wept on him and yelled: "O poor pa!" So Freddy got Mr. Bean aside and told him what had happened. "Can't you get rid of them?" Freddy said. "Can't you tell them to go?"

Mr. Bean shook his head. " 'Tain't possible, her bein' my wife's cousin. And we promised. We've just got to keep 'em and make the best of it." He hesitated a minute, puffing on his pipe so that the smoke completely hid his face. Then out of the smoke cloud came his voice: "Though, o' course if *you* was to think of something—"

When Mr. Bean hid in a cloud that way it meant that he was through talking to you. So Freddy turned away.

But Mr. Bean called after him. "Don't try

anything till you get back from Mars, though. Uncle Ben's all set to leave Friday—mustn't disappoint him. He says it means waiting another eight months if he don't start Friday—Mars won't be in the right place the rest of the year. We can hold out all right.''

It was the first time Mr. Bean had really appealed to Freddy for his help, and Freddy knew that he would have to do something. But it would be several months at least before he got back from Mars, and he didn't know whether the Beans could really hold out that long or not. For the Bismuths ate so much, and did so much damage that he didn't think there would be any Bean farm left if they stayed a few more months. Only the day before, the two Bismuth children, Carl and Bella, had smashed all of Mrs. Bean's wedding china. They had climbed up on the pantry shelves to get at a glass of crabapple jelly, but Carl had slipped, and the children and the shelves and the jelly and a hundred and twenty-one pieces of Ironstone china had all landed together on the pantry floor with a most terrific crash. And as always, when the Bismuths had an accident, they had a good one. There was only one unbroken saucer left in the whole set, and that one Bella dropped and smashed when she picked it up and carried it out into the kitchen to show Mrs. Bean.

Freddy had a talk that evening with his partner in the detective business, Mrs. Wiggins. Cows are not generally thought to make good detectives; they are too big and noisy to be much good at shadowing suspected persons, and they're not usually much interested in doing anything but just standing around and being cows. But Mrs. Wiggins's strong point was her common sense. She had solved a good many cases by just being sensible. Many detectives, and other people who have problems to solve, could do well to follow her example. She was of course well known and very highly thought of by others in the profession and she could have walked into any detective agency in the country and got a job.

She agreed with Freddy that there was nothing much he could do about the Bismuths until after the Mars trip. "But I'll keep an eye on them," she said. "Trouble is, Mrs. Bismuth being Mrs. Bean's cousin. Mrs. Bean has got such strong family feeling that she'd be mad at us if we did something really mean to them."

"So would Mr. Bean," Freddy said. "He was awful mad at Hank the other day for pushing Carl into the watering trough. He said Carl hadn't done anything to deserve such treatment."

"Hadn't done anything! Land sakes, ain't just being a Bismuth enough?" Mrs. Wiggins demanded.

"Well, I guess ducking the boy wasn't so much what Mr. Bean was mad at as shoving him back in three times when he was trying to get out. I guess Hank got kind of excited, because he didn't really want to drown Carl. Hank's pretty soft-hearted, really."

They talked late, trying to work out some plan for keeping the Bismuths from making too much trouble while Freddy was away. Then they discussed poetry for a while, and Freddy recited several little things that he had recently dashed off. And he was just saying good night when Quik and Eeny, two of the mice, came galloping into the barn. They were yelling and whooping with laughter, and if you think a mouse can't make a lot of noise you should have heard these two. "Oh boy!" they shouted. "Oh golly, Freddy, wait till you hear this one!"

"Well, O K," said Freddy. "Tell it, and quit the racket." And Mrs. Wiggins said: "Good grief, you boys ought to be home under the stove in bed, not tearing around all over the neighborhood keeping decent people awake!"

Eeny was rolling on the barn floor with laughter, but Quik got hold of himself and stood up and frowned at the cow. "All right," he said crossly. "All right—you want to hear it or don't you?" Quik was even more touchy than most mice.

So Freddy and Mrs. Wiggins said sure, they wanted to hear it; and Mrs. Wiggins even woke up her two sisters, Mrs. Wurzburger and Mrs. Wogus, who had got pretty sleepy during the latter half of the evening (cows haven't much feeling for poetry), and they gathered around Quik.

"Well," said Quik, "you know about Mr. Gridley's hitting old Bismuth on the nose today, and bending it around farther to the side than ever. A couple more pokes like that and Bismuth'll be breathing into his own left ear. Well, anyway, when they were getting ready for bed tonight Mrs. Bismuth says: 'Ed,' she says, 'you got to do something about your nose. It's

twisted around so far now that when you blow
it you have to stand almost behind yourself.
And when you're walking around your nose
ought to point the way you're going, not off at
right angles. It confuses people.'

"So she gets out some rubber bands and hooks
'em over his right ear and then over the end of
his nose, so they'll pull it around straight.
'There,' she said, 'now if you'll sleep with that
on for a few weeks I guess it'll go back where it
belongs.'

"So old Bismuth, he grumbles a while, but
then he goes to sleep—at least he starts to, but
when he wiggles his head down into the pillow
one of the bands slips off his nose, and smack!
—it hits Mrs. Bismuth right in the eye!"

Eeny, who had sobered down a little while
Quik was talking, began to giggle again. But
Freddy said: "How do you know all this? You
talk as if you'd seen it."

"Sure we have," Quik said. "We've got a nice
new hole gnawed up into the spare room. It's
in the corner under the dresser, but please don't
tell Mrs. Bean, Freddy. We've promised not to
gnaw around the house, except a few places

down cellar where it doesn't matter. But the Bismuths—my gosh, Freddy, they even eat in bed—take cookies and cake and pie upstairs with them. And there's crumbs everywhere. Gosh, you could feed a regiment of mice with what drops on the floor.

"Well anyway, that's how we saw what went on; we were up there having sort of a late snack before going to bed. So when the rubber band hit her in the eye, Mrs. Bismuth thought Mr. Bismuth had hit her, and she began to holler and cry; and then he jumped up and another band pops off and hits her in the other eye—boy, oh boy, we like to died laughing!"

"Yeah," said Eeny, "only Cousin Augustus had to go and get the hiccups like he always does when he's excited, and they heard him and got up and poked after us under the dresser with a coat hanger. We got away all right, but the hanger hit Eek—he's got a peach of a black eye."

"I hope they don't find that hole," said Quik. "Mrs. Bean will be awful mad."

"I wish we could plug the hole up," Eeny said. "But you can't un-gnaw a hole, I guess."

"If there's any trouble about it," Mrs. Wiggins said, "you can tell her about the rubber bands. Mrs. Bean likes a joke, and if you get her to laughing, she'll forget to be mad."

"Maybe she'll be so mad she'll forget to laugh," said Eeny.

"Just show her Eek's eye," said Freddy. "I think a mouse with a black eye is funnier than all Mr. Bismuth's rubber bands."

"Yeah?" said Eeny crossly. "Somebody else's black eye is always funny. I'd like to see you with one, pig."

Freddy grinned. "Pick on somebody your size, mouse," he said. Then he yawned. "Well, I'm for bed. Goodnight." And he trotted off towards home.

CHAPTER
5

During the next few days, before the departure of the space ship, the Bismuths were pretty quiet. Partly it was because the little Bismuths were sick. Between them they had eaten nearly five pounds of the candy their father had brought them. And partly it was because Mr. Bismuth went down to Centerboro every day. Mr. Bean had lent him the $35 to pay back the seven people whose money he had spent, and he paid them and went around explaining to everyone how the whole thing had been a joke, and he hadn't meant to steal the money. He was a good explainer. A lot of the people believed him. All except Dr. Wintersip. When he went to explain to the Doctor, the door was slammed in his face. If his nose had been straight, the door would have taken the end of it right off. As it was, it missed it by a good inch.

Freddy had to spend a lot of time in the men's furnishing department of the Busy Bee, getting fitted to a space suit. The Busy Bee had a good line of space suits, but they were for people, and they had to be cut down and altered a lot to fit animals. The suit for Charles of course had had to be specially made, as even a cut-down boy's suit will not do for a rooster.

Early on the morning of the day set for the take-off, all the animals for miles around came pouring through the barnyard and up the slope to the pasture where the rocket stood. Georgie and Robert, and half a dozen dogs from neighboring farms whom Uncle Ben had hired for the job, acted as police, and kept the crowd back of the fence that surrounded the pasture. For there would be a big blast of flame and hot gases when the rocket was fired, and it would be dangerous to be anywhere near it.

A lot of people had come up from Centerboro, too. Mr. Bismuth had built a small grandstand at the north end of the field, and was charging ten cents for seats; but he hadn't done a very good job on it, and when six or seven people climbed into it the whole thing collapsed and came down with a crash. He said that it fell down because he hadn't had enough money to buy nails for it, and had had to use old rusty bent ones he found in the barn. But Mr. Bean said that there were plenty of nails in it; the trouble was that they were all put in in the wrong places.

Fortunately nobody was hurt, though one of the prisoners from the jail—the sheriff had given them the day off to go see the rocket fired—had his new derby hat smashed. He made such a fuss, threatening to call the state troopers and make Mr. Bismuth buy him a new hat, that Mr. Bean promised to buy him one. It cost Mr. Bean seven dollars.

The rocket was to take off at eight twenty-one. Uncle Ben with his passengers—Jinx and Charles and Freddy and Georgie—had been aboard since five o'clock. Only Mrs. Peppercorn had not yet put in an appearance when, at eight o'clock, Freddy stepped to the doorway of the ship and addressed the crowd.

"Ladies and gentlemen," he said, "we are, as you know, taking off in a very few minutes in this, the Benjamin Bean Space Ship, with the object of reaching and exploring the planet Mars. Mr. Benjamin Bean has asked me to say a few words in explanation of just how we plan to do this. In order to get through the earth's atmosphere and out into space, it is necessary to start with a speed of at least 25,000 miles an hour. Needless to say, until the invention, by Mr. Benjamin Bean, of the Benjamin Bean Atomic Engine, no such speed was possible. But with this engine, now for the first time installed in a space ship, Mr. Benjamin Bean states that he will be able to develop a velocity, not of 50,000, but of 100,000 miles per hour! (Loud cheers.)

"What does this mean, ladies and gentlemen? It means that instead of taking six months to reach Mars, our ship will reach that planet in about a week. It means further that—" He stopped suddenly. A car came bouncing and bounding up through the gap in the fence and swung around and stopped at the foot of the ladder. Judge Willey was driving. He hopped out and opened the door on the other side and a small figure in a space suit climbed stiffly out. In one hand this person held a large umbrella, in the other a small paper bag.

Freddy called: "Hey, Uncle Ben, Mrs. Peppercorn is here!" and then ran down and with the Judge's help hoisted the old lady up the ladder and into the ship. "She doesn't have to wear this suit," he panted; "not until we land on Mars," and Judge Willey panted back: "She wanted to show herself off in it. That's why we're late. Made me drive her all around town. You'd think she'd been elected queen. Bowing and waving to the populace."

Freddy went down and started to go on with his little speech, but Uncle Ben came to the door. "Zero minus five," he said. "Get in."

So Freddy got in and they shut the door and spun the wheels that locked it tight. "Lie down on the floor," said Uncle Ben. With his eye on his watch, he kept one hand on the big valve that controlled the Benjamin Bean Atomic Engine. And when the watch showed exactly eight twenty-one, he spun the valve.

There was a terrific roar, and the floor seemed to come up and press so hard against them that they could barely draw breath. For a few minutes the pressure got worse and worse as the big rocket built up speed. Then slowly the pressure diminished, and soon they were coasting. They were outside the earth's atmosphere.

At first, when the ship was building up more and more speed in order to leave the earth, Freddy had felt as if he weighed a ton. He felt as though, if he weighed just one pound more, he would squash himself out flat against the floor. But when the rockets were cut off and the ship was coasting, he got lighter and lighter, and the first thing he knew he didn't weigh anything at all. He rose right off the floor and began to drift around the control room along with the others, who of course were doing the same thing. Presently he bumped into Jinx.

"Hi, pig," said the cat; "fancy meeting you here!"

Uncle Ben was steadying himself by holding on to the padded hand rail that ran around the

"Hi, pig. Fancy meeting you here."

room. He was watching the radar screen. "Catch hold of the rail," he said. "Help Mrs. P."

Mrs. Peppercorn had let go of her umbrella while she was struggling to get out of her space suit, and it had floated off. She was making sort of swimming motions to catch up with it, but every time she managed to touch it it would move away from her. Jinx and Freddy tried to help her, but the umbrella seemed to be alive; it was rather like three swimmers trying to catch a live fish under water. It was Charles who got hold of it finally with his beak. By using his wings he was able to move about more freely than the others.

Mrs. Peppercorn thanked him, and they had all gathered by the big window and were looking out at the black sky, sprinkled with thousands and thousands of bright points. There wasn't much to see. The earth was behind them and so was the sun; Mars was still on the other side of the sun, swinging around in its orbit towards the spot where they planned to meet it. Uncle Ben pointed out Venus and Saturn and some of the big fixed stars. Of course they didn't really need the window; in order to navigate the ship they had the Benjamin Bean Large Economy Size Radar Screen, which would give them all the information they needed.

They were discussing this when Uncle Ben held up his hand. "Listen," he said. They stopped talking. At intervals of perhaps six seconds there came a little sound: click . . . squeak . . . click . . .

"It's inside the ship," said Georgie.

"Of course it is, you dope," said Jinx. "There's nothing outside except the universe."

"Better find it," Uncle Ben said. For if one of the instruments had gone wrong, or if there was a leak of some kind, things could be pretty serious.

So they began hunting. They floated around, looking behind things and under things, and Uncle Ben took several of the instruments apart and peered into them. But still the click continued.

"You're just wasting your time, young man," Mrs. Peppercorn said finally. She always called Uncle Ben "young man," although he was forty-seven years and two months old. "There's nothing in here that clicks. It must be outside. And if there's nothing outside but the universe, then it's the universe that clicks. Although if a uni-

verse the size of this one can't do more than
squeak like an undergrown tree toad, then it
ought to go out of business."

"The tree toad doesn't squeak," said Charles.
"It—"

"Hey!" Jinx interrupted. "Look!"

Since none of them had any weight, they were
all floating freely about the room, holding on
by the handrail, like swimmers clinging to a
raft. The space suits and all the boxes and
various objects that they were taking to Mars
were fastened to the floor or walls so that they
wouldn't get in the way; but a few had been
loose, and although Uncle Ben had captured
and tied most of them down, a large heavy box
was drifting around right in the middle of
the room. It contained bright bead necklaces,
lengths of red cloth, and trinkets of various
kinds, which Freddy planned to trade with the
natives of Mars for whatever they had that was
of value. Now, out from behind this box, a
small animal floated. A mouse. He was waving
his paws feebly, trying to pull himself back out
of sight, but being without weight he was help-
less.

"A stowaway!" Freddy exclaimed. "Why, it's Cousin Augustus! How'd you get here?"

"Wanted to go to—hic—Mars," said the mouse. "I got in and hid a week ago. I'm—hic —I'm hungry."

Each hiccup twisted him a little in the air, so that as he talked he turned a very slow somersault. Of course, having no weight, there was no up nor down, and unless they were holding on to the rail, all of them were in different positions. Freddy thought it was fun, talking to somebody who was apparently standing on his head in the air. But Mrs. Peppercorn didn't like it.

"I wish you'd turn right side up so I can talk to you," she had said crossly once to Jinx.

"But I am right side up," he replied. "You're the one that's upside down." As of course she was, from his point of view.

"Isn't any 'up'," Uncle Ben put in.

"Fiddlesticks!" she snapped. " 'Up' is this way." She pointed a finger toward the space over her head.

But Uncle Ben, who was hanging on to the rail, reached out and gave her shoulder a gentle push, and she turned a slow half circle, so that her feet were where her head had been a second before. "Now where's 'up'?" he asked.

"Oh—oh, fudge!" she said disgustedly. Then she laughed. "All right," she said; "but for goodness' sake, Jinx, don't start doing cart-wheels again when you're trying to tell me something."

It was hard to tell what to do with Cousin Augustus. They stopped the hiccups with a drink of water and gave him something to eat. They couldn't just tell him to get out and go on back home, a couple of hundred thousand miles through empty space. Freddy said that stow-aways always had to work their passage, and Jinx suggested that perhaps they could send him outside to wash the window. Of course Jinx wasn't serious, because even if the mouse had had a space suit, there was no way of getting him out and in again, but the mere thought of going out into emptiness brought back the hiccups. At last Uncle Ben tied him to the rail with a piece of string and set him to keeping an eye on the radar screen.

And the rocket whizzed on towards its meeting with the planet Mars.

CHAPTER

6

There isn't much to do on a space ship. Except for watching the radar screen and occasionally regulating the temperature and pressure, there is no work for the crew. There wasn't much to see out of the window, either. The stars were brighter and there were millions of them, but as Cousin Augustus said, when you'd seen one, you'd seen them all.

After the first day, the novelty of not weighing anything, of not knowing whether they were on their heads or their heels, had worn off. Among the trade goods which Freddy had brought was a checker board, and he and Mrs. Peppercorn tried to play; but the checkers wouldn't stay on the board. They floated an inch or so above it, and if you happened to brush one with your hand it would drift off, and when you went after it the others would swim around and get all mixed up.

It was impossible to believe that the ship was moving away from the earth at 100,000 miles an hour. It was hard to believe that it was moving at all. Indeed Mrs. Peppercorn refused to believe it. She said if she opened the door, she'd be able to climb right down into the Bean pasture. "We haven't moved an inch," she said. "This ship isn't taking us anywhere. I'm going to get out and go home." Fortunately she wasn't strong enough all alone to turn the wheel that sealed up the door.

Freddy spent a lot of time sleeping. You

didn't have to lie down to go to sleep. You just closed your eyes and floated without touching anything. It gave Jinx nightmares, though, to sleep without feeling any bed under him. It made him dream that he was falling, and he'd wake up with a screech. Finally Uncle Ben tied him to the rail with some strips of cloth, so that he could feel something solid against him, and he slept better.

Freddy wrote one poem, but it was so much fun to let go of the pencil and see it stay right there in the air with its point on the paper, that it wasn't a very long one. It went like this:

Hark
  While I croon a verse
In praise
  Of the universe.

The universe is quite good-sized,
And is, I think, well organized,
Containing as it does, a slew
Of stars and planets. Comets too
Occasionally whiz about
And dodge and circle in and out
Among the clustered nebulae.

They scare the dickens out of me,
But I suppose they know their stuff
And are expert and quick enough
To keep from bumping or colliding
With other worlds. But I'm residing
At present on the planet, earth,
And it does not arouse my mirth
To see these reckless comets fly
Around as if they owned the sky.
It's much too dangerous in a crowd,
And really shouldn't be allowed.
Yet tho there's nothing to prevent
Bad manners in the firmament,
The heavenly bodies, generally,
Are well behaved and courteously
Avoid all quarrels and disputes—
Tho when they have them, they are beauts.

As to the universe's size,
It's rather large than otherwise,
Containing stars and galaxies
And satellites of all degrees.
And some are dim and some are bright
But all are lighted up at night,—
Mostly along the Milky Way—
A quite remarkable display.

Some scientific fellows hope
By peering thru a telescope
To chart the heavens and name each star
Of all the billions that there are.
More sensible I think it is
Just to sit back and let them whiz
Along on their accustomed track
Around and round the zodiac.
For since they are not bothering me
I think it's best to let them be.

And that is all I have to say
About the universe today.

Freddy might have written more, but when she found out what he was doing, Mrs. Peppercorn remarked that as a girl she had been no slouch of a poet herself, and she kept trying to help Freddy. Some of the verses were pretty terrible. Here is one:

"Some stars are large and some are small,
And some are quite invisiball."

And another went like this:

"The light from some far distant stars
Does not reach earth for yars and yars."

She was quite irritated with Freddy when he wouldn't put them into the poem.

Luckily they were able to talk with the earth. Uncle Ben had built a radio outfit; there was a short wave transmitter on the ship, and another in the cow barn, which he had trained Mrs. Wiggins' sister, Mrs. Wurzburger, to run. She was to be on duty twenty-four hours a day. So they were able to find out everything that was going on at the farm, a couple of hundred thousand miles away.

At first there wasn't anything very exciting in the way of news. But on Sunday, Mrs. Wurzburger had some real trouble to report. It seemed that on Saturday afternoon Mrs. Wiggins had been invited to tea by Miss McMinnickle, who lived in a little house down the Centerboro road. She had a dog, Prinny, and you may remember that one of Freddy's first detective cases was known as "The Case of Prinny's Dinner."

The animals were often invited out like this —to tea, or to dinner, or to play cards in the evening. Mrs. Wiggins was very popular. It is true that like most cows she was rather clumsy, and in moving through a room, or in the excitement of an argument, she often knocked over small tables and other furniture, and occasionally a priceless vase or some other valuable knickknack got smashed in this way. But she cried so hard when she did anything like this, and was so well liked, that the owners always said it didn't matter.

On this afternoon, Mrs. Wiggins was sitting in Miss McMinnickle's front parlor, drinking tea and discussing various neighborhood topics with her hostess when Mr. Bismuth called. He was a frequent caller. Miss McMinnickle made a very rich and delicious fruit cake, and rich food drew Mr. Bismuth as syrup draws flies. He could be very entertaining when he wanted to, and Miss McMinnickle was always glad to see him.

But after her callers were gone, and she was brushing up the crumbs, Miss McMinnickle couldn't find her purse. She looked and looked, and at last when she was sure that it was not in the house, she called the state troopers. They came and searched the rooms in which the Bismuths were living at the Bean house and found nothing. Then they searched the cow barn. And tucked down in a corner out of sight, they found the purse. But the eighty-three dollars that had been in it was gone. They arrested Mrs. Wiggins and took her down to the jail and locked her up to await trial.

Of course the Beans and the other animals didn't believe for a minute that Mrs. Wiggins had stolen the purse. Even the troopers were pretty doubtful, for—as they said—they had never before even heard of any cow who was not a model citizen. They even called up J. Edgar Hoover and asked him if the F.B.I. had ever investigated a cow. But he said that in all the annals of crime there was no record of a cow criminal. But Miss McMinnickle was mad and demanded Mrs. Wiggins' arrest, and so of course she had to be put in jail until she could be brought before the judge for trial. She thought it was rather fun, herself.

Freddy was pretty worried. Not on Mrs. Wiggins' account: he knew that Judge Willey would never pronounce her guilty. And he knew too that the sheriff, who was a friend of his, would make her stay at the jail a pleasant one. But

They arrested Mrs. Wiggins.

now there'd be no one to keep an eye on the Bismuths.

"But Mr. Bean won't stand for any monkey business," said Georgie.

"He won't if he can help himself," Freddy said. "But the only way to keep out of trouble would be to tell the Bismuths to get out. And he won't do that, because you can't throw your cousin out in the street."

"You can't, hey?" said Jinx. "I'd throw my whole family—cousins, sisters, aunts, grand-mothers—the whole kit, cat and caboodle—right out on the sidewalk if they started crowding me out of my own house, the way these Bismuths are doing. You know what their latest caper is? They want Mr. and Mrs. Bean to give up their nice front bedroom to Carl, so he can put up a pingpong table there. Mr. Bean said why not use the loft over the stable, but Mrs. Bismuth said it was draughty, and Carl was too delicate —he might get pneumonia. Pneumonia—ha! I pity any germ that tackled that kid!"

"But Mr. Bean won't let him have the room, will he?" Georgie asked.

"Oh, my goodness," said Freddy, "you know how it'll be. He'll say no, of course; but they'll keep on squalling and begging, and Mrs. Bismuth will burst into tears at the breakfast table—"

"After her fifteenth pancake," put in Cousin Augustus.

"Yeah," said Jinx. "And Bismuth, he'll say how 'twon't really be giving up anything, because the little back bedroom is much handier to the kitchen, and so on. And by and by the Beans will give in, just so the Bismuths will shut up. That's the way it's been about everything else—Bella always having a pitcher of cream with her cereal, because she's delicate, and old Bismuth having chicken every meal because he's delicate, and Mrs. Bismuth always sitting in the parlor while Mrs. Bean cooks the meals and washes the dishes—because she's delicate too. Why, they're all so darned delicate that they can't manage to eat but six or seven meals a day."

But until they got back, there wasn't much they could do to help the Beans, whom they were leaving behind them at the rate of 100,000 miles an hour.

They usually tied themselves to something before going to sleep. The first night they hadn't known they needed to, and they drifted around the control room like dust specks in a sunbeam, until Charles drifted into Freddy. The pig was just taking a deep breath when it happened; he drew in Charles's tail feathers with the air, and the rooster, dreaming that he was being swallowed by an alligator, turned with a squawk and clawed and pecked at Freddy's nose. It took them all an hour to settle down again.

It was on Sunday night, when they were all asleep except Georgie, who was on watch, that they had a bad scare. Jinx came loose from his rail and drifted into Mrs. Peppercorn, who waked up with a yell when she felt a small cold nose in her ear. She struck out excitedly with both hands; she didn't hit the cat, but somehow managed to turn a valve that controlled one of the small side rockets which were used to steer the ship. And at once the ship began to spin.

Now of course everybody in the ship spun with it. But it didn't seem to them that they were spinning; it seemed, when they looked out of the window, as if the whole universe was spinning around them. Stars and galaxies and constellations swept past, and then the sun, in a blaze of light, and then more stars. They seemed to be the center of a million whirling lights . . . and then Uncle Ben got to the controls, cut off the rocket Mrs. Peppercorn had fired and turned on one that stopped the spin.

"Dear me," said Mrs. Peppercorn, "that was a very pretty display. Rather like the fireworks that the Centerboro Chamber of Commerce shoot off on the Fourth. Though not, of course, as well managed."

"I expect these large scale things are rather harder to manage," said Charles drily.

Uncle Ben shook his head. "Hope we ain't been thrown off our course. I kind of lost direction for a while." He looked out of the window, then after peering for a while at the radar screen, made a few entries in his notebook. "If I ain't miscalculated, Mars should be directly ahead," he said. "Three more days in that case. We'll see."

But the next day he pointed out the planet they were aiming to head off as it swung along on its orbit around the sun. It didn't look as if it was moving, but they knew that it was really tearing along at terrific speed. Of course their speed was even greater, for they had to follow it hundreds of thousands of miles as it swung around the sun, in order to catch up with it, and land. It didn't get much bigger for another forty-eight hours, and then all at once it began to grow. In an hour or two it grew from the size of the moon until it filled up half the window.

"Where are the canals?" Freddy asked. "I thought there were canals on Mars."

"Looks sort of like the map of Europe," said Georgie. "You know—where Spain sticks out on the southwest corner."

"Clouds, probably," Uncle Ben said. "Stand by now. Going to turn the ship around and start braking with the big rocket for the landing."

This was a complicated operation, but Uncle Ben fired a steering rocket and the ship swung around so that its base was towards the planet. Then he fired the big rocket. And all at once they had weight again; the floor pressed up against them as it had on the take-off. Slowly Uncle Ben brought their speed down until they were going only a little faster than the planet. They couldn't see their landing place through the window, which looked up now towards the sun; Uncle Ben had to judge his distance from the ground by his instruments. Then their weight decreased, and with a jarring thump they landed.

CHAPTER

7

As soon as the rocket landed, they got into their
space suits and prepared to explore their new
world. There was no suit for Cousin Augustus,
so he got inside Freddy's. He sat on the pig's

shoulder so that he could look out through the wide plastic helmet. Since the atmosphere on Mars contains no oxygen, each suit had a small cylinder which would supply enough oxygen to last the wearer two days, and each suit had a Benjamin Bean Improved All-Purpose Walkie-Talkie, so they could communicate with one another.

When they were ready Uncle Ben unsealed the door and threw it open, and they looked out on a world that was all black and grey, a dead world. They had landed in what seemed to be a forest of black spikes, gnarled and twisted, many of them, into queer shapes. The ground was black—it was as if volcanic fires had seared and blasted everything which might once have been living. And over it all the rain poured down.

They had decided that Mrs. Peppercorn, being the only lady in the group, should have the honor to be first to set foot on the new planet. A space suit is nearly as difficult to move around in as a diver's suit, and as Mrs. Peppercorn insisted on putting her umbrella up as soon as she was through the door and starting down the ladder, they had a lot of trouble getting her down to the ground. "You don't need an umbrella," they said. "Your suit's waterproof."

"If I've brought this umbrella all the way from Centerboro to Mars," she said, "I'm certainly not going to leave it stand in a corner when it rains."

Finally they rigged a line under her arms and lowered her, and she started off with the umbrella held over her head.

"Better stay near the ship," Freddy called after her.

She didn't even turn around. "I want to have a chat with some of those educated spiders you told me about," she said, and cackled with laughter as she stumped off among the black spikes.

"Hope she don't meet anything worse than educated spiders," said Freddy. "But it's no use trying to stop her."

"Are the Martians really like spiders, Freddy?" Cousin Augustus asked. He was hiccupping slightly from nervousness.

"Nobody knows what they're like," said the pig. "They may be forty feet tall, or they may be like insects, or they may—oh, my goodness, they may be big snakes with wings, or sort of land octopuses with long tentacles and two foot beaks—"

"Oh, stop it! Hic—stop it!" Cousin Augustus exclaimed. "I'm scared enough without you making all these horrid things up."

"Well, of course maybe Mars isn't inhabited at all," said the pig. "Maybe it's all like this, a sort of burnt up desert. We may be the only living things on the whole darned planet."

"Maybe 'tain't Mars anyway," said Uncle Ben. "Maybe we're somewhere else. Venus. I dunno." He was puzzled, for after Mrs. Peppercorn had put the ship into a spin Sunday night he had lost direction for a while, and hadn't been quite certain just whereabouts in the solar system he was.

However, after taking a sight on the sun, which was just about to set, and making some more calculations in his notebook, he said: "Must be Mars. Ain't any other planets in this part of the sky except maybe Venus, and she's closer to the sun than what our earth is, so she'd be hotter."

"She doesn't spin as fast as the earth and Mars do either," Freddy said, "so her day would last about two hundred fifty hours, instead of twenty-four. That means that in the hour since we've landed the sun wouldn't have moved so you could notice it. But it's a lot lower now than it was."

"That's right," Uncle Ben said. "I ought to thought of that. Yep, we're on Mars all right. That's a big relief to me. Ain't no place to be losing your way, out in the middle of the solar system."

They walked around for a while as the daylight faded. There wasn't much to see in the forest of black spikes. The thing to do, they decided, was to get the ship all ready for a sudden take-off, in case they were attacked by Martians; then to have a good night's sleep, and do their exploring in the morning. They could see nothing of Mrs. Peppercorn, but Freddy spoke to her over his walkie-talkie and told her she'd better come back.

"Oh, stop bothering me," she said crossly. "I'm busy. Something going on here, and I want to see it."

"What is it?" he asked. "Shall we come?"

"No. Stay where you are. I'm hiding behind a tree and watching."

"Behind a what?" Freddy exclaimed.

"A tree!" she snapped. "T-r-e-e, tree! Good heavens, don't you know what a tree is?"

"Sure," he said. "But if there are trees on Mars . . . What kind of tree?"

"How do I know?" she demanded. "There ain't any label on it. It's got leaves and a trunk and there's ants walking up and down it. One of 'em just bit me."

"Ants!" he said.

"If you can't do anything but repeat every word I say, I'm going to shut this talkie thing off," she said angrily. "I want to see what this man is up to."

Freddy started to say: "Man!" and then stopped himself. "But there aren't any men on Mars," he said. "There can't be."

"There's one," she said. "I'm looking at him. He's walking along—sort of sneaky—and looking into the creek."

"Creek!" The word popped out before he thought.

Mrs. Peppercorn made several remarks about Freddy's brains, and then she calmed down and told him that the man was some distance away, and that it had got so dark in among the trees that she couldn't see him very clearly, but he

"There is one," she said.

had two legs and two arms and a head, and certainly looked like a man. He had something over his shoulder—a gun, or a shovel. "But there's something following him, I don't know what it is," she said. "It walks along quite a ways behind him and it isn't more'n a foot high. It's got something over it, a dark cloth—maybe a kind of raincoat, with a hood. It's got two legs, and it's got big bright yellow shoes on."

"Wow!" Freddy exclaimed excitedly. "I wish you'd taken a camera. Must be a Martian. You hear that, Uncle Ben? Little man a foot high with big feet."

"He's got kind of a beak, seems like," said Mrs. Peppercorn. "Or else he's got a big pipe in his mouth that sticks out under the hood."

Freddy asked if they were making noises of any kind.

"Don't be silly!" she said. "I don't think they're together; the little one's watching the big one. Anyway you know you can't hear anything inside these helmets. All nonsense, wearing the things, anyway. I'm going to take mine off—see if I can hear anything."

"No, no!" said Freddy. "You mustn't! You won't last two minutes if you do. This air on

Mars isn't like the air at home; it's poisonous."

"Fiddlesticks!" she exclaimed. "Air's air. And that man doesn't wear a helmet."

"He isn't a man, he's a Martian," said the pig. "Probably doesn't need oxygen. Probably hasn't even any lungs—" Freddy stopped, remembering suddenly that she couldn't get the helmet off by herself anyway, since all the helmets were fastened by nuts, which had to be screwed down from the outside.

"Oh!" she said suddenly. "He's starting this way. Guess I better come back."

They watched, and pretty soon saw her come stumping along, still holding the umbrella over her head. The Martians evidently weren't following her—at least there was no sign of them.

When she had been helped back into the ship she told them that she had come, after a few minutes' walk, to the end of the black spikes. Here were woods, with trees exactly like those on earth, through which a brook ran. There had been no signs of life, though, until the appearance of the man-like creature and its queer little companion. She thought the man one had caught sight of her; he had suddenly got behind a tree and started moving stealthily towards her.

The explorers had thought it wise, in case they had to defend themselves, to bring along Mr. Bean's shotgun, and a big old fashioned six-shooter that Freddy had taken away from Signor Zingo, the circus magician, two years earlier. They got these out and loaded them, and when they had eaten supper, Uncle Ben said he and Freddy would take turns standing watch while the others slept.

It was during Freddy's first watch, about nine o'clock, that the only suspicious incident occurred. It was a clear night, but of course the stars did not give much light. For a quarter of an hour Freddy thought he had seen movement of some kind among the stubs a little way off. Then he was sure of it. He couldn't hear, inside the helmet, but there was a gadget that he could switch on so that he could hear outside noises. He turned the switch now, and at once he heard a faint rustling, as of someone creeping nearer. He snapped the gun to his shoulder and fired both barrels.

As the boom of the gun died away, he heard what sounded like the thump of footsteps, running. He heard something else, too—a faint swishing sound in the air above his head, and then from the direction in which the footsteps had gone, first a couple of deep-toned hoots, and then a sort of yell. He knelt down at the foot of the ladder and hurriedly reloaded.

The bang of the gun had waked everybody up, and after a few minutes he climbed into the ship to report. "I may have hit that man-like thing," he said, "but I don't think so. He'd have yelled when I hit him; he wouldn't have waited nearly a minute. It wasn't human, that yell!"

"Maybe he was calling other Martians," said Georgie. "Maybe they'll attack at dawn, like the Indians."

Freddy told them about the sounds that had preceded the yell. "I'm sure that some big creature flew over my head," he said. "Maybe it pounced on that man creature—that's why he yelled. It was—golly, it must have been enormous, the swishing it made. Like one of those old dinosaurs, with wings."

"You said it hooted," said Jinx. "Like an owl?"

"If you can imagine an owl as big as an elephant," said the pig. "It was deeper, like a steamboat whistle."

Cousin Augustus got the hiccups so badly at

this point that Freddy had to stop talking for a while. He climbed down again and took up his post at the foot of the ladder. But nothing further happened that night.

CHAPTER

8

The next morning it was sunny, and leaving Georgie in charge of the ship, the explorers set out. After ten minutes or so they came to the end of the forest of black spikes, and sure enough, there were trees and a brook, just as Mrs. Peppercorn had said, and beyond, green fields with what looked very much like earthly grass growing in them. There was no sign of the Martians. They went across the brook and spread out some of their trade goods—bright bead necklaces, and shiny pocket knives, and alarm clocks, and lengths of red cotton cloth— on the grass. Then they crossed back and hid among the trees and waited.

They waited all morning and nothing happened.

"Maybe they're too scared of us," said Jinx.

"Well, we're scared of them, so that makes it even," Freddy said.

"They're probably like the Indians when they first saw white men," Mrs. Peppercorn said. "You shouldn't have shot at them. You ought to have gone out and shaken hands with them."

"Oh, yeah?" said Jinx. "I didn't notice you exchanging any hugs and kisses with them last night."

"Anyway," said Freddy, "maybe they're more civilized than we are instead of less. Maybe we're the Indians and they're the white men."

"Atom guns," said Uncle Ben. "Death rays."

"That's right," said Freddy. "Maybe they could just turn a little switch and bang! we'd all fall to pieces."

Mrs. Peppercorn was poking at the ground with the ferrule of her umbrella; suddenly she leaned down. "My land," she said, "here's a four leaf clover!" She picked it and held it up.

"Funny," said Uncle Ben. "Everything just like earth. Trees, clouds, clover—everything. Must be careful."

"That's right," Freddy said. "We mustn't forget that it *isn't* the earth. We mustn't forget that this air isn't really air at all, and probably the water in this brook isn't really water, either. If we just—"

He stopped suddenly, for Georgie's excited voice came through— "Listen! Listen! Mrs. Wurzburger just phoned. There's a flying saucer or some kind of space ship landed, just up north of the farm. She's been out watching for invaders; that's why she didn't let us know before. It landed yesterday."

"Funny they'd land on earth the same day we land on Mars," said Cousin Augustus.

"Oh, pooh!" said Freddy. "She's kidding us."

"No she isn't," Georgie said. "Mr. Bean saw it land. He's posted some of the animals along the edge of the woods on guard duty, and he's phoned the other farmers and the troopers and everybody."

"Are they looking for the ship?" Jinx asked.

"They don't dare. They don't know what kind of weapons these other-world beings may have. Mr. Bean says, no shooting: try to keep everything friendly."

"Phooey!" Charles exclaimed. "Keep everything friendly indeed! That, my friends, is not a counsel that *I* would give, were *I* there!" He began to strut up and down. He hadn't made a speech in some time, and this seemed like a good chance. "What! will they bow the knee to these invaders?—will they surrender the broad lands of Bean without a struggle? Not so would I do. Before I would see the homes of my friends ravaged and the torch put to my own ancestral henhouse—"

"Oh, button your beak, rooster," said Jinx irritably. "If you weren't all done up in that plastic suit I'd put the torch to your ancestral tail feathers. You wouldn't talk so big if you were there."

This was not strictly true. Charles always talked big. As a speechmaker he was in great demand, not only on the farm, but even in Centerboro, for Rotary and Chamber of Commerce dinners, and so on. Partly, of course, it was the novelty of being addressed by a rooster that made his human audiences applaud; but partly too it was his fiery eloquence. There was only one trouble with his speeches—nobody could remember afterwards what they had been about.

He went on now at some length, disregarding Jinx's remarks, about the defense of the homeland.

From Charles' own point of view, the great trouble with his speeches, particularly the patriotic ones, was that they had a much greater effect on him than on his hearers. Ordinarily he never picked fights, but after making one of his speeches he was so excited and warlike that he would pitch into any animal that so much as grinned at him.

Freddy realized this. He didn't want Charles inciting the others to attack the Martians; they were in danger enough without that. But before he could make any attempt to calm the rooster down, Jinx said excitedly: "Look! Look!" And down along what looked like a stone wall, two fields away, came walking the strange little creature with the big yellow shoes that Mrs. Peppercorn had described to them. It was alone, and had evidently not caught sight of them.

Before they could stop him, Charles stepped out from their hiding place and began shouting defiance. The Martian, however, paid no attention—which was not surprising, since the rooster was doing all his shouting inside his helmet, and could be heard only by his shipmates.

But Charles was not accustomed to having his words disregarded. And nothing is more insulting than to have your own choicest insults met with blank indifference. Without stopping to wonder why this was so, he gave a squawk of sheer rage and charged out into the open field at the little Martian.

Jinx and Freddy got up, but Uncle Ben told them sharply to stay where they were. "Rooster's a fool," he said. "Must take his chances."

"But he's our friend," Freddy protested.

"Yeah," said Jinx, "and if we go back without him and Henrietta hears we didn't stand by him—boy! I'd rather be scalped by Martians than face that hen when she's mad. Come on, Freddy." But then he paused. "Oh-oh! Guess we aren't needed after all." For the little Martian had at last caught sight of Charles and started to run.

Charles ran after him. It wasn't a very exciting chase. Charles was hampered by his heavy space suit, and his usual swift run became a series of clumsy hops. But slow as he was, he was overtaking the other, whose bright yellow shoes seemed to be so much too big for him that he kept stepping on his own feet as he waddled hastily towards the woods, half a field away.

"That little guy sure isn't Olympic material," said Jinx. "I guess Charles can handle him."

The Martian, who had already fallen over his own feet several times, now fell again, just as he reached the shelter of the trees. Charles was right behind him. What he intended to do wasn't very clear, for he could use only his feet and spurs as weapons, since his beak was inside the helmet. But before he could do anything, something swooped down upon him—a great bird, it looked like, but in the shadows under the trees they couldn't really make out what shape it had. And it snatched Charles up and flew off with him. For a little while they heard over their walkie-talkies his frantic cries for help. Then there was silence.

The Martian had disappeared, but they were too horrified to notice. It was the last they would ever see of an old and tried—and sometimes, of course, very trying—friend. Of that they were sure. Even Uncle Ben was saddened by the catastrophe, though he and Charles had never been very close. Mrs. Peppercorn, however, made no bones about the satisfaction she felt.

"Noisy, gabby critter," she said; "good riddance, I say. Place for him is on a platter with a dumpling tucked under each wing, but if the Martians are smart, they'll parboil him all day first. Boil some of the oratory out of him."

Jinx had said some pretty harsh things about Charles at various times, but this made him mad. "Oh, yeah?" he said. "Well, if the Martians catch us, I'll see that they roast you over a slow fire. Though I'm sorry for the guy that takes the first bite. I hope he knows a good dentist."

and it snatched Charles up. . . .

"No way to talk to a lady," said Uncle Ben reprovingly.

"Well," said Freddy, "it isn't really any way for a lady to talk about our friend, who has just been carried off to a horrible fate by a whatever-it-was. What do you imagine it was, Uncle Ben?" he asked, thinking it would be tactful to change the subject.

"Dunno." Uncle Ben shook his head. "Mebbe the big critter that whooped, last night."

"Sort of like a dragon," Freddy said. "Golly, I hope there aren't a lot of those things around." He glanced apprehensively towards the trees where Charles had disappeared. "No use chasing that little guy with the shoes now. Hadn't we better go back to the ship and hold a—well, a sort of council of war?"

Georgie's voice cut in on them. "You can't get back now. The ship is surrounded. I've just shut and locked the door. The Martians are all around me. What 'll I do, Freddy?"

CHAPTER

9

Back on the Bean farm there was a good deal of worrying going on, and Alice and Emma, the two ducks, were certainly doing their share. They had reason to. It had all started the day of the fire, when the Centerboro engines had pumped so much water out of the pond, and with it a great deal of the rich nutritious mud on which they depended for their three meals a day. At first they had been almost sick with worry, for not only was the mud gone, but they feared that with it had vanished all their family jewelry.

To speak of ducks having family heirlooms in the shape of rings and necklaces and brooches may seem odd, and it will no doubt surprise many people to learn that most ducks have quite a tidy fortune in jewels concealed in the bottoms of streams and ponds. Mostly these are things that people have dropped out of boats, though Alice and Emma had also a number of very handsome pieces that Uncle Wesley had collected in his travels. Among them, and perhaps the pride of the collection, was a string of a hundred and eighteen matching pearls with a ruby clasp which he had picked up one day while having lunch in a swamp near Syracuse.

For a time the ducks had kept these treasures in the vaults of the First Animal Bank, of which Freddy was President. But an attempt to rob the bank, though unsuccessful, alarmed them, and they had returned the jewels to the bottom of the pond. When so much of the mud had been pumped out with the water, they feared that the jewelry had been sucked out with it; but the pumper had worked at the northwest end of the creek, the jewelry, hidden near the outlet at the southeast end was, when they looked for it, undisturbed.

But after all, as Emma said, what good were pearls and diamonds when there was nothing to eat in the pantry? Now when they dived, their broad bills scraped along the bare stony bottom.

Uncle Wesley's letter in the newspaper however had brought one result: Mr. Bismuth had read it and come to see him. There had been several conferences—what they had discussed Alice and Emma had not found out. But they were worried, for their uncle had gone off with Mr. Bismuth and had not been seen for two days. It was the day after he had left that the report came in that a ship full of wild-eyed and ferocious creatures from another world had landed a few miles north of the farm. Alice and Emma shook their heads sorrowfully over it. "Poor Uncle," Alice said, "it would be just like him to try to capture these dreadful people single-handed."

"I know," said Emma. "He would have been too proud to hide from them. I have sometimes wished that he was not *quite* so courageous."

They were both sure that the pompous little fraud had died a hero's death.

But nobody so far had seen anything of the visitors from outer space. The state troopers refused to take any stock in the report that a space ship had landed; they wouldn't even go look for it in the woods north of the farm. "It's just another of those flying saucer yarns," they said, when Mr. Bean insisted that he had seen it himself. "If these things have landed on the earth, where are they?"

Mr. Margarine, however, the city man who owned the place just west of the Bean farm, had seen the ship, and he and his chauffeur, and Mr. Bean and Zenas Witherspoon and the Macy boys and some of the other farmers patrolled the woods, armed with rifles and shotguns. They had all seen the ship, or claimed to, but they hadn't ventured very close to it.

It was John, the fox who spent his summers

At this point Emma fainted.

on the Bean farm, that told the ducks of having seen one of the visitors. "I was up in Witherspoon's pasture," he said, "and I looked
over towards the woods—it was raining and I
couldn't see very well—but this thing came out
to the edge of the woods. It looked—well it
looked more like a toadstool than anything, although it had legs and walked on 'em."

"How dreadful!" said Alice, and Emma mur-
mured faintly: "Oh, mercy!"

"It looked as if it was made of dark metal,"
John continued. "Or maybe it is the stuff ants
and beetles are made of, shiny and black—"

At this point Emma fainted.

When Alice had brought her round, John
had discreetly left.

And then two days after Uncle Wesley's
disappearance, the brook that fed the pond
stopped running. It stopped as abruptly as if
someone had turned off a faucet, and when the
water had all run out the other end the bottom
lay exposed and drying in the sun. The mud at
the outlet end dried and cracked, and here and
there in the cracks you could see the yellow of
gold or the flash of a diamond.

The ducks just sat on the bank and cried, and

the tears ran down each side of their yellow bills and splashed on the grass. But at last Alice sat up and dabbed at her eyes with a burdock leaf. "Come, sister," she said; "this is unworthy of us. What would dear Uncle Wesley say?"

"He would say what he always said," Emma replied: "that we were a pair of silly females. That we just sat down and sniffled when we ought to be up and doing. And he was right, sister."

"He was always right, dear Uncle Wesley," said Alice. "Be up and doing—that was his motto."

"Yes it was, sister. But—" Emma hesitated. "Well, we're up, but I don't know what comes next. What could we be doing that would be any good? Oh, I do wish Uncle were here!" And she began to cry again.

"Now, now," said a voice behind them. "In trouble? Tell old Bismuth all about it. Yes sir —ha, ha!—Bring your troubles to Bismuth; he'll straighten 'em out for you."

The ducks had heard enough about Mr. Bismuth to suspect that people who brought their troubles to him just exchanged them for worse ones. Also, they were much too ladylike to dis-

cuss private affairs with anyone except their
uncle—which may explain why their affairs
were often so badly snarled up.

But Mr. Bismuth knew what the trouble was
without their saying anything. "Water, eh?
Gone to make mud somewhere else, I guess.
Well, that's an easy one. If you want mud, mud
won't come to you, so go where the mud is.
Hey? Well, come along; I'll show you."

The ducks didn't really believe that he was
going to be much help, but when you say
"mud" to a duck it's the same as saying "ice
cream" to a boy. So they followed him across
along the southern edge of the woods a ways,
then down towards where in a little depression
in the meadow Mr. Bean had planted a vegetable garden. Only now, instead of vegetables,
there was just water. It had made a pond out
of the garden. It flowed in as a new little brook
that came out of the woods, and at the lower end
it flowed out again, joining the old bed of the
brook a little farther down.

"Why this is dreadful!" Alice exclaimed.
"All Mr. Bean's lovely vegetables! Oh, dear
me!"

"But this must be our brook," said Emma. "How did it get over here?"

"Don't anybody know," said Mr. Bismuth. "No, sir; some say one thing and some another. Some say the brook got tired of running in the same old channel and kind of struck out for itself. Ha, ha! Went explorin', like. And other folks, they think that the fishes in the brook were the ones got tired of swimmin' up and down between the same old banks, and just started off cross lots, and the water had to follow 'em."

Alice and Emma didn't like to be teased, especially by a comparative stranger like Mr. Bismuth. "There is no need to insult our intelligence with silly stories," Emma said with dignity. "If you don't know, kindly say so."

"I apologize, I apologize," he said. "A Bismuth will have his joke, you know—ha, ha! Sorry if it displeases you. Matter of fact, nobody knows what happened to the brook. Some think these flying saucer folks changed its course. Maybe we'll find out if we ain't all killed in the next day or so."

Emma said: "Oh, dear!" in a faint voice, but

Alice said: "Perhaps you can tell us, sir, if there is any news of our Uncle Wesley. He went away with you, we believe. Did he return with you?"

"Wesley? Wesley?" Mr. Bismuth looked down at the ground frowning, as if in deep thought. At least that was the impression he intended to give, though with his nose twisted so far to the left he looked, as Alice said afterwards, rather as if he was listening to see if he was going to sneeze. "No," he said. "Don't remember the name. Your uncle, you say?" But before they could protest he pulled out a large nickel watch and examined it. "Dear me, I'm afraid I'm late. Should have been there an hour ago. Bismuth's always absent-minded, very. Ha, ha! Excuse me, ladies." And he turned and hurried off.

"Well, that's very abrupt, I must say," Alice remarked.

"A most offensive manner, with his ill-timed witticisms," said Emma. "I know what Uncle Wesley would say."

Alice nodded. "Yes. Hardly a gentleman, I think dear uncle would feel. Yet I suspect that he knows something. Well, sister, I suppose we can only wait. And meanwhile—dear me, it's very uncomfortable on this dry grass. Of course Mr. Bean wouldn't like to have us in his garden, but it's scarcely a garden now, is it? I really don't think he'd mind." And she waddled down into the water. After looking around rather doubtfully, Emma followed her.

They swam around for a while, and dove to explore the bottom. "I can't say I care for this new mud," Alice said. "Such an odd flavor."

"It does taste queer," Emma agreed. "Not really the sort of thing we're used to." She came up a minute later with a limp tomato plant in her bill. "Oh, poor Mr. Bean!" she said. "His lovely garden, all drowned. You know," she said, "in a way I'm relieved that Uncle Wesley isn't here. I just found a—forgive me for mentioning it, sister—an angleworm." They both shuddered delicately. "Not that I mind them, really—I suppose they're quite nourishing. But you know how particular he was about his food. Merely the thought of one made him quite ill."

A deep voice in the tree overhanging the pool said sarcastically: "Just how I feel about him, pompous little squirt."

The ducks looked up and saw old Whibley, the owl, perched on a lower branch.

Emma said hufflily: "You would not dare speak slightingly of Uncle Wesley, were he here to defend himself."

"Well, why isn't he here?" said Whibley. "Pistols for two in the cold dawn, hey? Fine! I'll fight a duel with him—any weapons he chooses: pistols, swords, war clubs, coke bottles, or just beaks and claws. Well, where is he?"

"You are very bold," said Alice, "when you know quite well he is not here."

"Went off with old busy Bismuth, didn't he?" the owl asked. "D'you know where they went, or why? Or what they were having all those conferences together about?"

"We see no reason why we should answer these questions about Uncle Wesley's private affairs," said Emma. And Alice said: "Indeed, they are highly improper."

"Oh, be yourselves!" said Whibley impatiently. "I know the answers. I'm just trying to find out if you do. Because if you do, you're in trouble. Same as your silly old uncle. You—"

"I think we do not have to listen to this, sister," said Emma with a toss of her head. The ducks turned their backs and swam off.

"Oh, wait, wait!" Whibley called after them.

"Don't be so darned ladylike.—Oh, all right," he said as they continued to move away from him. He dropped from the branch and floated on his big silent wings across over their heads. "If you and old Wes got Bismuth to monkey with the brook, and bring it down here so you'd have more mud, you're going to have Mr. Bean in your hair. Or in your feathers. Which will probably be stuffing one of the spare room pillows by next fall." His wings beat lazily and he drifted off towards the woods.

Emma turned anxiously to her sister. "What do you suppose he meant? Do you think Mr. Bismuth really changed the course of the brook?"

But Alice just tossed her head old maidishly and said: "I don't think *anything* he could say would be worth listening to. Not after those slighting remarks about Uncle."

"No, I suppose not," Emma agreed. "He's always so sarcastic. I suppose it comes from sitting up so late nights."

They paddled along, quacking quiet agreement that the owl was indeed rather an undesirable character, and certainly a bad example to the younger animals on the farm.

CHAPTER 10

Back in the space ship, Georgie felt pretty much alone. As soon as he had seen figures moving stealthily among the black spikes around the ship, he had reported to his friends, and at their suggestion had closed and locked the door.

"We can't get back to the ship while you are being besieged," Freddy said, "but I think maybe we can drive the Martians away. After dark we'll try some of the Big Bangs. That ought to scare 'em off."

Among the things that they had brought along to trade with the Martians were several dozen of the Benjamin Bean Increasingly Loud Explosive Alarm Clocks, known as "Big Bangs" to the trade. This clock was one of Uncle Ben's less successful inventions. It shot off a series of firecrackers at two minute intervals, each louder than the last—the idea being that a light sleeper would be roused easily by the first mild bang, a heavy sleeper by some later and heavier bang, and the really lazy person, who kept turning over after each bang and trying to go to sleep again, would be lifted right out of bed by the final bang, which was a jim-dandy. The only trouble with the clock was that frequently the final bang blew it to pieces, scattering little brass wheels all over the bedroom. And nobody wants to buy an alarm clock that can't be used more than once. So Uncle Ben had a lot of them on his hands.

Now they picked up the Big Bangs, leaving

the other trade goods where they were spread out on the grass, and crept cautiously back towards the ship. They had gone only a little way when Georgie's voice came again into their ear phones. "Mrs. Wurz. just phoned again," he said. "She says the brook—you know, the one that comes down through the woods into the duck pond—well, it has stopped running into the pond and it's coming down along the west side of the woods and flooding Mr. Bean's garden. It's going to spoil all the vegetables. They think those flying saucer people did it, but they don't know why. Some think the farm will be attacked next."

"I think we ought to get home," Freddy said. "We mustn't let Mr. Bean down. And since the Martians don't seem to want to trade peaceably, we'll have to come back again with more guns and things. We can't fight 'em with what we've got."

Uncle Ben nodded agreement. "Claim it first," he said. "Put up flag."

"That's right," said Jinx. "We ought to take possession of Mars for the United States. Boy, won't that be something? I bet it'll make old What's-his-name look sick—Columbus. Golly, he just discovered half a world; we discovered a whole one."

"We've got to try to rescue Charles first, though," Freddy said. "I don't think they've eaten him. If they've never seen a rooster before they wouldn't know whether he was good to eat or not."

"Cook him right in that suit," said Mrs. Peppercorn—"that's what I'll tell 'em to do if I see them. Make him nice and tender, even a tough old chicken like him."

"Don't ever call him a chicken," said Freddy. "It makes him mad. —But come on, let's get these Big Bangs in position."

Georgie reported that the Martians had not come close to the ship; they were hiding among the black spikes mostly to the south and the east of it. Though they had apparently posted sentinels in a circle around it.

"Like men?" Uncle Ben asked.

"Well, some of them have got two legs," said Georgie, "and some four or five. They're very— well, they seem to be all sizes. Haven't seen that little thing with the yellow shoes anywhere."

For the next few hours they lay concealed in a fold of the ground not far from the ship. It seemed as if it would never get dark, but at last it did. They set the Big Bangs to go off all together in ten minutes, put them in a line facing the ship about five yards apart, and then hurriedly circled around to the south side and waited.

The plan worked perfectly. The clocks exploded their first firecrackers in a sort of irregular volley. In two minutes came the second ripple of fire, louder this time, as if the attackers were coming closer. But it wasn't until the third firecrackers went off that the Martians began to reply. They had weapons of some kind, which flashed and banged very much like earthly shotguns, and two or three small searchlights were turned on to hunt for the source of the firing.

Of course they didn't find it, and when the alarm clocks had all shot off their third firecracker and were silent for two minutes, the Martians stopped shooting too.

"If they don't charge the Bangs, or else turn and run, we won't be able to get back to the ship," Jinx said.

"If they're anything like us," Freddy said, "they'll have to do one or the other. Their nerves won't let 'em stand still when they're be-

The other Big Bangs began firing their final shots.

ing attacked by enemies that keep coming closer and closer, and still they can't see them. Wait till the last bang."

But the Martians had better nerves than Freddy had thought. They replied to the fourth volley, and after it, continued to search with the beams of their spotlights. Luckily for the explorers, just as the fifth and final round of firecrackers were ready to explode, one of the alarm clocks was spotted, and held in the beam of one of the lights.

"Hey, look!" Jinx exclaimed. "Boy, that ought to give those Martians the wigglies! Look, they're turning all their spots on it! Golly they're looking for a bunch of snipers sneaking up, and all there is is one little lone alarm clock moving in on 'em."

And at that moment the clock blew up. Bang! went the fifth firecracker, and the bits of glass and tin and little brass wheels glittered in the light as they went whizzing off in all directions. And bang, bang bang!—the other Big Bangs began firing their final shots.

This was too much for the Martians. The spotlights went out, but before they did Freddy could see dark figures break from cover and run. They ran past the ship and when he turned on his outside microphone to listen, he heard footsteps dying away to the westward. "All clear, Georgie," he said. "Unseal the door, we're coming aboard."

They made the ship without any further trouble. It seemed certain that the Martians would not bother them again for a while, so they decided to hold a short ceremony and annex Mars to the United States. As the first of all earthly creatures to set foot on the new planet, Mrs. Peppercorn was chosen to take possession of it for her country. She tied a small American flag to the handle of her umbrella, then climbing down the ladder to the ground thrust the ferrule of the umbrella into the blackened earth, and said in a loud voice: "In the name of the Bean Family, the Peppercorn family, and the Continental Congress, I take possession of this here planet, and claim it as the sole property of the United States of America, with all its continents, rivers, mountains, lakes and canals; with all its seas, oceans, forests, deserts, and other appurtenances, wherever and howsomedever located and arranged; with all its inhabitants, whether men, animals, birds or bugs; whether smart or dumb. And I further declare that later, if and when it is admitted to statehood, it shall be known as the State of Peppercornia, and—"

"Hey wait a minute," Jinx shouted. "If we're going to name it, let's put it to a vote. I vote for Jinxia."

"Why not call it Georgia?" said the dog.

"There's a Georgia already," Cousin Augustus objected.

"New Georgia, then."

"Voting's no good," said Freddy. "We'd each vote for his own name and be right back where we started. Why shouldn't we call it New Beanland, after Uncle Ben and Mr. Bean?"

"Beanland indeed!" said Mrs. Peppercorn. "Let me tell you, young man, that the Peppercorns settled half this country before the Beans had got down out of the trees. If the Peppercorns had had their rights, one—yes, perhaps two or three of the original thirteen states would have been named after them." And she went on to make a speech about the distinguished past of the Peppercorn family which even Charles could not have matched for eloquence.

But in the end she was voted down. Mars became New Beanland.

Now at this point, if Freddy had not thought he saw a light moving about some distance off, in the direction of the meadow where they had left their trade goods spread out; if they had got back into the ship and fired themselves off into the sky, in an effort to return to earth—well, goodness only knows what would have happened to them. It is doubtful if they would ever have been seen again around the Bean farm.

But Freddy did see a light. And he thought: "If we could only capture a Martain and bring him home with us—golly, then we'd have *proof* we'd been to Mars. That's what Columbus did —he brought some Indians back to Spain. Nobody'd have believed him if he hadn't."

He didn't tell the others what he intended. He knew they'd object. He just said: "I'll be back in a few minutes," and started out.

The stars gave some light, and it was not as dark among the spikes as it would have been in regular woods; but because the ground was black Freddy fell over a good many things before he came to the edge of the open land. Fortunately the Martian didn't hear him. He was very busy tying up the trade goods into a big bundle, and the noise of the brook, near which he was working, covered the sound of Freddy's stumblings. Evidently he intended to make off with the things before anyone else could get them.

Freddy crouched behind a bush and watched for a few minutes. The Martian looked exactly like a man, though he seemed to have no face—at least when he turned Freddy's way there was nothing but a white blur under the brim of his hat. Freddy loosened the big pistol in its holster and was preparing to jump out and try to capture him, when he suddenly heaved the big bundle on to his back and started off down along the brook. Freddy followed.

Pretty soon the brook turned in among the black spikes, but the Martian kept on in a southerly direction. He climbed a wall and crossed what seemed to be a road—Freddy couldn't see it, but he could feel hard packed earth under his feet. Then the Martian turned towards the west and in a few minutes put down his bundle on the lip of what appeared to be a hole in the ground a little bigger than the Bean barnyard.

But when he jumped down in, Freddy saw that it was a depression only about three feet deep.

The Martian started digging with some sort of a small tool like a trowel, and Freddy crept closer. He was pretty scared. He had never captured anybody before and didn't know how to go about it. He could point the pistol and threaten to shoot. But suppose the Martian didn't know what a pistol was? "Would I have to shoot him?" he thought. "But I don't want to shoot anybody." And then he thought, suppose the Martian had some kind of an atom ray gun and all he does is point it at me and pop! I'm just a little heap of dust. He got quite worried about this gun and even found a name for it— the Practical Disintegrator. But that didn't make him feel any braver.

He lay there on his stomach and watched the Martian dig, and he said to himself: "Freddy, I don't believe it's a very good idea capturing this fellow. There isn't really room for him in the ship, and when you get him back to the earth, what are you going to do with him?"

So then he answered himself, and said: "Well, I suppose we could keep him tied up in the box stall in the stable. But what do Martians eat? Maybe we wouldn't have the right food for him, and he'd get sick."

"Yes," he said, "and anyway this is really kidnaping, and that's never a nice thing to do."

"It's a crime," he replied. "Golly, maybe they could send me to prison for it."

He nodded his head, and said seriously: "Look, Freddy, this is something you want to think about pretty carefully before you do it. You might get in a lot of trouble."

"Yeah," he said. "But the only thing is—if you come back to the ship without him, will somebody say you're a coward?"

"I don't see why," he answered himself. "You just said you'd be back in a minute, you didn't say you were going to capture anybody."

"That's right," he said. "Anyway, your reputation is too well known for anyone to accuse you of being afraid."

He nodded his head several times, and then he said: "Well, you've convinced me. I guess it wasn't a very good idea." And as both of him were now in agreement he decided to leave.

He had pulled out the pistol; now he started to shove it back in the holster. But it caught, and in tugging at it he pulled the trigger. It went off with a tremendous bang.

Just what happened to the Martian Freddy didn't see, for the shot made him jump, the lip of the depression where he was lying gave way, and he fell sprawling into what was evidently a mudhole where the Martian had been digging. When he got up and wiped some of the mud off his helmet, the Martian had apparently run away. But between the darkness of the night and the mud, he was practically blind. And now when he looked around, he could see the flicker of lights some distance off, and they seemed to be moving nearer.

"I'd better get out of here," he thought, and started back the way he had come. But the lights came rapidly closer; it was impossible for him to outrun them. He turned, drawing the pistol again out of its holster. But before he could make out anything even to point the gun at, three or four flashlights were focussed on him, and then he was seized and thrown to the ground; a rope was wound tight around him; and then he was forced again to his feet and dragged off like a dog on a leash.

He could see nothing of his captors, and he couldn't reach the button to turn on his outside microphone, to find out if they talked together. All he could do was speak to his friends and tell them that he had been captured. He made quite a noble speech. "Do not attempt to rescue me," he said. "It is for me to suffer the penalty of my own folly; it is for you to leave me to my fate, however horrible it may be; it is for you to return to earth with the glorious news that a new world has been discovered; for me to pay the price of the discovery. And I do so gladly. Go then, my friends, for home, for country, and for Bean; go and fulfill those high hopes with which we set out—ah, how short a time ago. My blessing goes with you. Farewell, a long farewell."

But he was pretty sure that they would try to rescue him.

CHAPTER

11

Freddy's captors did not take him far. They led him along for a couple of hundred yards, and having tied him to a tree, focussed their flashlights on him and began asking questions. At least he supposed they were asking questions, for though he could see nothing with the lights in his eyes, and could hear through his helmet only a confused gabbling, now and then one of them would shake him as if trying to shake an answer out of him. But they didn't hurt him or abuse him, and after a while they went away.

Although he was tied to the tree, Freddy wasn't specially uncomfortable. But he was pretty worried. Of course he had no way of knowing what sort of things Martians ate, but he had an idea that almost everybody was fond of roast pig. Several times in the course of his career as a detective he had been in danger of being baked, fried or roasted. And then, if the Martians didn't eat him, they might keep him prisoner; and he had no way of getting a fresh supply of oxygen. He wouldn't be able to last more than a day longer.

He was engaged with these gloomy thoughts and wishing that he hadn't made that noble farewell speech, so that he would have an excuse for appealing to his friends for help, when dimly through the mud on his helmet he caught the flicker of an approaching light. It came closer, then someone began wiping the mud off the outside of his helmet. When this was done, the light was held on his face for a long minute. Then it went out and he felt someone untying the ropes.

The figure looked like a man; if it was one of his friends, it must be either Mrs. Peppercorn or Uncle Ben. "Thank goodness you've come," he said.

Georgie's voice answered. "Freddy! What do you mean? For Pete's sake, where are you? We didn't know which way you went, so we couldn't come after you."

Freddy's heart sank. If it was Uncle Ben who was untying him it would be his voice that came through the walkie-talkie, not the voice of Georgie, back in the ship.

He explained what had happened. "But don't—repeat, *don't* try a rescue. I think I can get back without help."

I suppose this was the bravest speech Freddy had ever made, and in the course of his adventures he had made quite a number. But though the speech was brave, he didn't feel very brave inside. His tail in fact had come completely uncurled, as it always did when he was scared. For though Freddy was brave, he was not fearless;

indeed most apparently fearless acts are done by people who are just shivering inside. That's what bravery usually is.

Jinx and Georgie and Mrs. Peppercorn all started talking at once, but Freddy said: "This Martian is untying me. He seems friendly. Probably we can't talk, but I guess I can tell something by the sounds he makes, so I'm cutting out the walkie-talkie and switching on the outside mike, so he and I can hear each other. I'll cut you in again as soon as I can."

The Martian had loosened the ropes; now he turned off his flashlight and tapped Freddy lightly on the shoulder. It seemed to be an encouraging tap, so Freddy said hesitantly: "How —how do you do?"

The Martian made a funny sort of fizzing noise, but didn't say anything.

"Maybe that's the way Martians say How do you do," Freddy thought. He said: "Oh dear, I wish you could speak English!" And then, speaking very slowly and distinctly, he said: "Do—you—understand—English?"

The Martian fizzed again, and then he said, spacing his words as Freddy had; "Guess—I— kin—manage—it—if—you—speak—real—slow."

It was surprising that the Martian could use human speech; it was amazing that he could speak English; but it was almost incredible that he could speak just the kind of New York State English that Freddy and his friends always spoke. Of course he spoke it very slowly, and he fizzed a lot between words, so that Freddy wondered if he was some kind of mechanical man, run by an engine.

Well, they had quite a talk. Mostly the Martian asked questions and Freddy answered, relating the story of their journey through the solar system. He didn't say anything about their having annexed Mars to the United States, for he didn't want the Martians to think that the Americans would take away their independence.

Now and then a second voice put in a question, so that Freddy was aware that another Martian was present, though of course he couldn't see him. And it was this second one that asked a question that astonished Freddy even more than the good English that he used. "And when you set out on this journey," he said, "how did you leave my good friend Mr. Bean?"

"Mr. Bean!" Freddy exclaimed. "But how—how could you know about Mr. Bean?"

The voice gave a deep chuckle. "Visited your country many times. Know Bean, know Schermerhorn, know Witherspoon. Very fine country. Martians may take it over some time. Know about you, too. Know about the time you shot a snake in the old Grimby house in the Big Woods, and it turned out to be an old rope. Know about your falling headfirst into Dr. Wintersip's rain barrel—"

"But you—you couldn't!" said Freddy. "Why, that was only the other day!"

The deep chuckle came again. "Was in Centerboro the other day myself. Don't believe me, hey? Well, must take you for a drive in my new flying saucer. These new nineteen fifty-four models, with supersonic drive, fingertip control, automatic stardust dodger and all the rest of it—as you say on earth, they're *something!*" The first Martian began making such loud fizzing sounds at this point that he stopped.

"Is he talking Martian to you?" Freddy asked.

"Martian? Er—ha! Hum! Yes." The question seemed to embarrass him. Then he said: "Matter of fact, he wants me to show you who I am.

There sat the owl, old Whibley.

Better prepare for a shock. Because I live part
of the time on earth—up in the Big Woods, in
fact; and you've talked to me a good many
times. A light, if you please, Mr. Er—uh . . ."

The beam from the flashlight came on and
swung around up into the tree above them,
and Freddy gasped. For there sat the owl, Old
Whibley, who did indeed live in the Big
Woods.

"But this—it's impossible!" Freddy stammered. "You—well, for one thing, you couldn't
breathe this air on Mars."

"But I do breathe it," said the owl. "It's good
air, contrary to what people on earth have
always supposed. Take off that helmet; I'll
prove it."

"No!" Freddy yelled. "No! I will not! You
must think I'm crazy."

"All right, all right," said Whibley irritably.
"I never argue with lunatics. If you like to walk
around with a kettle over your head, go to it."

"But I have to," Freddy insisted. "If this is
Mars, the air would poison me in a—" He broke
off. "Hey, what am I saying! *If* this is Mars—
If! But *is* it? Say, look! Let me see who that is
with you." For it suddenly came to him that the

fizzing sound the other Martian had made was very familiar. It was exactly the sound Mr. Bean made when he laughed.

And sure enough, the light swung down and there in the beam was Mr. Bean's face, with a broad grin on it, probably, though you couldn't tell behind all those whiskers. But he was fizzing.

Freddy's mind was putting two and two together at top speed. The night when the space ship had spun around, and Uncle Ben had been afraid that he might have lost his way and be headed for the wrong planet. The landing in the forest of black spikes—which might be—what? A burned-over area on some other planet? But the trees, which were so much like earthly trees. And the four leafed clover. A burned area on earth? Or—good gracious—in the Big Woods?

"Looks like you've got it," said Mr. Bean. "Take off the helmet; we want to talk to you."

Freddy unscrewed the nuts that locked the helmet, then lifted it off—and he and Cousin Augustus took a good long breath of earthly air. "Then—then Uncle Ben did get mixed up after all?" he asked. "Got turned around and aimed back at earth instead of Mars?"

"Must have," said Mr. Bean. "You came down in the Big Woods, not a hundred yards from the Grimby house. Not half a mile from where you started. Hope you had a nice ride." And he fizzed some more.

"Yes," said Freddy. "But—well, I'm pretty confused. Is Charles all right?"

"Making speeches to the Martians, likely," said Mr. Bean. "Bein' Martians, they don't understand English, so probably they get about as much out of what he says as I do." And he fizzed some more.

"Oh my goodness, Whibley," Freddy exclaimed, "was it you that grabbed Charles and flew off with him? I thought it was some kind of a Martian dragon."

"Leave it to you to make a good story," the owl grumbled.

"Oh, all right, all right!" Freddy said irritably. "So I thought you were a dragon. So Uncle Ben aimed for Mars and got turned around and landed us back plunk! right where we started. I suppose if you'd been along, everything would have turned out all right!"

"Well, no," said Whibley mildly. "I guess I'd have thought we were on Mars, too. Matter of fact, when I heard you'd landed in the Big Woods, I thought what everybody else thought: that one of these flying saucers from some other planet was paying us a visit. But I was investigating Bismuth—he was up to something we'll tell you about later—and when I had a look at you I knew who you were. I was following him the other night and when you shot at him and he ran—I guess you heard him yell." The owl gave his steamboat whistle laugh. "I swooped down and tweaked his nose—I've been wanting to get a yank at that nose ever since he's been around here."

"But there was something following him," Freddy said. "Looked like a dwarf in big yellow shoes. Charles was chasing it when you snatched him up."

"Dwarf with yellow shoes, hey?" said Mr. Bean, and he fizzed like a leaky steam boiler. "That's a good one! Don't you worry about him, we know *who* he is, although we don't know right now *where* he is. Well, we got kind of a scheme we want you to try. Tell him, owl."

CHAPTER
12

When Old Whibley had recognized Freddy, the evening the rocket had landed in the burned-over part of the Big Woods, he of course realized at once that Uncle Ben had miscalculated. For the explorers showed by their actions that they thought they were on Mars. But he didn't tell them where they were, partly because he thought they were funny, clumping around the Big Woods in the uncomfortable clothes and stuffy helmets, thinking they were in great peril on a distant planet, when the only real danger was that they might fall down and bump their noses.

Except when he was called on for advice, Old Whibley seldom mixed much in the affairs of the farm. But when any serious danger threatened, he would take action. The Bismuths seemed to him a serious danger; if they were allowed to stay on, it would mean bad trouble for everybody, from Mr. Bean down to the smallest chicken in the henhouse. With Freddy away and Mrs. Wiggins in jail, there was nobody who could plan any kind of a campaign against the Bismuths—although there were plenty of animals who would be eager to take part in such a campaign. Mr. Bean, of course, would do nothing because Mrs. Bismuth was Mrs. Bean's cousin. Old Whibley got pretty impatient with him, and even told him so—which is more than any other animal on the farm would have dared to do.

But Mr. Bean just shook his head. "They're family," he said. "What's going to happen to 'em if I tell 'em to go?"

Whibley didn't say what he would like to see happen to them. He didn't even let on that he knew about the conferences that Mr. Bismuth was having with Uncle Wesley, although the result of them was to be the flooding of Mr. Bean's garden. And for some time he didn't tell Mr. Bean that the rocket that everybody thought was a flying saucer from outer space, was really Uncle Ben's rocket. But when he found that Uncle Ben and his crew all believed that they had landed on Mars, he went to Mr. Bean again, told him all he knew, and got him to agree to a plan for getting rid of the Bismuths.

"Don't like it," Mr. Bean had said. "Don't like plotting against my wife's relatives, and specially don't like playin' tricks on my wife. She'll be awful mad. But this tarnation Bismuth!— you're right, owl, we got to do something. Well, let's go get hold of Freddy."

Fortunately there was so much mud on Freddy's helmet when he was captured that Mr. Bean was able to manage it so that no attempt was made to see what he looked like, by offering

Good Gracious, that's outrageous.

to take him down to the farmhouse and lock him up; and after they had got no answers to their questions the other men agreed readily. None of them cared to take charge of a live monster from outer space, armed with goodness only knew what dreadful weapons.

It was of course dark when Freddy took his helmet off and looked around him, and he didn't at first recognize the mudhole where he had been captured.

"It's the duck pond," Whibley said. "One of Brother Bismuth's little jobs. Dammed the brook and then turned it into a new channel down the west side of the woods so that it flooded Mr. Bean's garden."

"Good gracious, that's outrageous!" Freddy exclaimed.

"That consarned duck, Uncle What's-his-name, got him to do it," Mr. Bean said. "Not enough thick muddy duck soup on the pond bottom since the fire. Well, guess Uncle's got good fresh vegetables in his soup now." He sizzled faintly with laughter.

"Must have been a lot of work for Mr. Bismuth, though, Freddy said. "He wouldn't do it for nothing. Did Uncle Wesley pay him?"

"Did it out of the kindness of his heart, according to him," Old Whibley said.

"Hey, wait a minute!" Freddy said. "When you grabbed me here, I was watching somebody dig in the bed of the pond. I thought he was a Martian. Why, that must have been Mr. Bismuth, and I bet I know what he was after!"

"Guess you're right," said the owl. "The jewelry that Alice and Emma kept there. Everybody knew they did; because Wes was always bragging about how valuable it was. Bismuth knew about it—"

"Yes, sir," said Freddy excitedly, "and I bet he was scheming to drain the pond and get it from the beginning. And when Uncle Wesley began hollering about the mud being gone, Bismuth jumped in and offered to help by changing the course of the brook."

"And he's got the jewelry; we were just down there looking for it," Whibley said. "Never mind that now. Mr. Bean and I are the only ones that know that Uncle Ben's space ship is right back here where it started from. Everybody else thinks you came from another planet, and that we've captured one of you. Now suppose that you pretend that that's so." And he went on and outlined their plan.

It wasn't much of a plan. It was to bring Freddy down to the farmhouse as a guest from Venus or Mars or Neptune. "We're sure that Bismuth has got that jewelry hidden somewhere," said the owl, "also the money he stole from Miss McMinnickle. You being right in the house, will be able to find it. Maybe even get him to tell you where it is."

"Yeah?" said Freddy. "How?"

"You claim to be a smart detective," said Whibley. "Well if you're so smart, figure it out. Don't make us do all the thinking."

"Don't you make me do it either," Freddy said. "Well, I'll try. I'd like to get him put in jail. But what would we do with Mrs. Bismuth and Carl and Bella the Yeller?"

So they talked about it for a while longer, and when Freddy had at last agreed, they started down to the farmhouse. But first Freddy talked to the space ship on the walkie-talkie. He told them just what had happened. To his surprise Uncle Ben didn't seem much disappointed. "Good thing," he said. "Not fuel enough." Which Freddy took to mean that if they had really been on Mars, there wouldn't have been fuel enough to get them back to earth.

But the others were not so well pleased, and Mrs. Peppercorn said that while she'd enjoyed the trip, she'd paid five dollars to go to Mars, and if this wasn't Mars, she wanted her money back. She was satisfied however when Uncle Ben said he'd take her on his next trip.

When Freddy told them what had been planned, they didn't like it at all. "Hey, look, pig," Jinx said; "you get all the fun, and what are we supposed to do—sit here in the woods and pretend we're Martians? Because we can't let people know we're back, or that this is Uncle Ben's ship—not while you're playing tag with old Bismuth."

Freddy referred this problem to Mr. Bean and Whibley. Neither of them had thought about it; nor did a solution occur to either of them now. Freddy didn't have any ideas either. So after a short consultation, he said: "We think that you'd better do nothing for twenty-four hours. We've got a plan, but we have to see how the first part of it works first. By tomorrow we can tell what will be the best thing for you to do."

Of course this didn't fool Jinx, who knew Freddy. "Oh yeah?" he said. "The same old wonderful plan you always have. I can tell you what it is in two words: stall 'em along."

"That's three words," said Freddy. "Anyway, Mr. Bean says to do nothing for a day. You want to argue about that?"

"No," said Jinx. "No. But see that you think of something before tomorrow."

So Freddy spent that night in his own bed in the pig pen, but he sent Cousin Augustus down to the house with instructions to tell all the animals to stand by to help him, and that he'd be disguised as a visitor from another planet.

The next morning he got out his make-up kit. It contained grease paints and false whiskers and such things which he used in disguising himself when being a detective. He thought for a while about what an inhabitant of another planet would look like, and decided finally that, as the creature wouldn't look like anything you'd ever seen before, it certainly ought to look as little like a pig as possible. So he painted his face blue and stuck a heavy black beard upright on top of his head, and he took the rat tail mustaches that he had worn as Snake Peters, the cattle rustler, and made eyebrows with them. He wore his space suit, but he left his helmet off.

After breakfast Mr. Bean came up to bring him down to the house. He walked out of the door and Mr. Bean took one look and started back. "Great earth and seas!" he exclaimed, and dropped down on the bench outside the door.

It wasn't easy to make Mr. Bean jump, and Freddy grinned and said: "Will I do?"

"Don't grin!" said Mr. Bean. "Too horrible. Do?" he said. "If you were any more so you'd scare me and Mrs. Bean away along with the Bismuths. You'd scare folks away for miles around. This here country would be a desert and waste. I dunno, Freddy; I dunno. Mrs. Bean has got strong nerves, but when she sees you comin' in the door . . ."

However, when Mr. Bean did bring Freddy in and introduced him as a man from Neptune, Mrs. Bean didn't even blink.

"H'm," she said; "pleased to meet you. I suppose, Mr. B., this is the gentleman who came in that flying saucer? Suppose there's no use my asking him if he had a nice trip."

"I haff—a—nize—trip—hat," said Freddy,

speaking very slowly in what he imagined might be a Neptunian accent. "I spik your lengwitch," he added.

"Lengwitch?" said Mrs. Bean. "Oh, yes—our language. Well now, that's very nice; we can have a good visit, Mr.—Mr. . . ."

"Captain Neptune, he says it is," put in Mr. Bean.

"I see. Well, Captain, we'll try to make your visit a pleasant one. Have you had your breakfast?"

"He doesn't eat breakfast," said Mr. Bean, who was afraid that if Freddy sat up to the table and ate he would give himself away.

"I like try—earthy breakfiss," said Freddy, with a reproachful glance at Mr. Bean.

"Good," said Mrs. Bean. "You just sit down in that rocking chair and I'll fix you some. Though goodness knows," she added, "there's little enough to fix it with. Those Bismuths finished up all the bacon and all the pancake flour this morning."

But pretty soon Freddy sat down at the table and ate hot biscuits and maple syrup and apple pie and coffee. And when he had finished Mrs.

Bean said: "Now Mr. B., you go do your chores and the Captain and I will have a nice long chat."

CHAPTER

13

Mrs. Bean asked Freddy a great many questions about life on Neptune, and from his answers she got the picture of a world very much like the earth. Neptunians lived in cities and worked in offices and factories, and in the countryside they had farms, where they kept animals: cows and horses and dogs.

"No pigs?" Mrs. Bean asked.

"Peegs?" said Freddy. "I not know ze peeg."

"Dear me," said Mrs. Bean, "you have indeed missed something. I am sorry our pig Freddy is away; you'd enjoy meeting him."

"He is small animals—so?" Freddy asked, indicating a creature about a foot long.

"Oh, no. Quite large and pink. Much too fat, of course. That's because he is so greedy. He's a very hearty eater."

"But is smart, ze peeg?" Freddy inquired. It seemed to him that Mrs. Bean might have thought of something nicer to say about him than how fat and greedy he was.

"Oh, he's smart all right," Mrs. Bean said, "but not as smart as he thinks he is. But he's a good pig, and we love him. He writes poetry."

"Po'try foolitch," said Freddy, shaking his head, and hoping that she would have something nice to say about his rhyming ability.

"Many people think so," she said, "but I don't agree. Of course, Freddy's no Shakespeare, but he's made some nice little verses.

Like the one—let me see, how does it go?'' She
thought a minute, then recited:

> *"I am smart and I am bright.*
> *When I do things, I do 'em right.*
> *There isn't anything I won't try.*
> *Oh, golly, I'm a brilliant guy!"*

Freddy sat up straight and stared at her. He
had never written those verses. It was true that
he often praised himself in his poems, but never
quite as shamelessly as that. Mrs. Bean must
have got him mixed up with somebody else.

He had come very near saying so, but remembered in time that he was Captain Neptune. "Good po'try," he said. "Is more?"

"Lots," she said, and recited another verse.

> *"People often praise some man*
> *Who I know I'm smarter than.*
> *What's he got that I ain't got?*
> *I admire myself a lot."*

Freddy was becoming more and more astonished. He had never written any such verse. He
wanted very badly to tell Mrs. Bean so, to as-
sure her that she was doing him a great injus-

tice in quoting as his such conceited lines. Why they didn't even scan.

Luckily at that moment Mrs. Bismuth and the two little Bismuths came into the kitchen for their mid-morning snack of cookies and milk. When she saw Freddy Mrs. Bismuth gave one of her loud emotional yells and fell fainting into a chair, and Carl and Bella gave smaller yells and ran out of the room.

Freddy had for the moment forgotten that he was made up to represent a Neptunian, and he was rather hurt at the effect his appearance seemed to produce. "These peoples crazy peoples?" he asked.

"Well, they're a little shy of strangers," said Mrs. Bean apologetically. "Excuse me, I shall have to revive poor Ambrosia." But instead of getting smelling salts, she went to the cupboard and brought out a large plate of cookies. These she began passing to and fro under the nose of the unconscious Mrs. Bismuth. And first Mrs. Bismuth gave a sniff, and then several more inquiring sniffs, and then her eyes opened and she sat up and a hand came out and seized a cookie. "Carl! Bella!" she called. "Where is your honored pa? Tell him, cookies!"

Within a minute the kitchen was full of Bismuths, wolfing down cookies and pouring milk from a big pitcher into glasses. And until the plate and the pitcher were empty, nobody paid any attention to Freddy.

Then Mrs. Bean said: "Ambrosia! Children! I want you to meet Captain Neptune. He commanded that flying saucer that landed in the Big Woods. We've asked him to stay with us."

"Where's he going to sleep?" Bella asked, and Carl said: "He ain't going to sleep in my front room."

"Now, now, children," said Mrs. Bismuth; "nobody's going to take your nice rooms away from you."

Well, Freddy knew that unless the Bismuths gave him one of the three rooms they occupied, there would be no place for Captain Neptune to sleep. And he knew that the Beans would never let a guest sleep in the barn. Which meant that they would give up their own room and probably sit up all night.

At this thought Freddy got mad. "Cap'n Neptune take *your* room," he said and pushed his ferociously grinning face close to Carl's.

A pig's grin is almost as terrifying as an alligator's, and when the pig's face is painted blue, and he wears a queer wig and eight-inch eyebrows, it is pretty horrible. Carl was too scared to yell; he just gave a sort of peep and flung his arms around his mother. Bella followed suit, although she yelled some; and Mrs. Bismuth yelled some too; and the kitchen was full of yells and weeping.

Just then Mr. Bismuth came in. He saw Freddy and said: "Whampo!" and fell back against the door. But he recovered quickly, and when he had stopped the noise by kissing Mrs. Bismuth and cuffing the children, he came over and shook hands with Freddy. "Heard about you," he said. "Happy to welcome you to the home of Bean and Bismuth."

"Bismut'?" said Freddy. "These house belong Bismut'?"

"Well, only in a manner of speaking, ha, ha," said the other. "But where a Bismuth lives is the Bismuth home. The Bean home, of course, too," he said tolerantly.

"Sometimes I wonder," said Mrs. Bean tartly.

"Pa," said Carl; "he can't have my room, can he?"

"You mean while he's staying here with us?"

Mr. Bismuth asked. "Why, it's very kind of you to offer it, my boy. Spoken like a true Bismuth."

Carl started to protest: "But pa, I didn't off—" when Mr. Bismuth's large hand, which had been patting the boy's head, slid down and covered his mouth.

"Very generous of you," his father went on. "But the Cap'n wouldn't want that room. Rattling windows, even when there's no wind— keep him awake. And the spiders! Oh, my, my, the great black spiders up in the southeast corner. Fangs just a-drip with poison as they come creep, creep down the wall, after you're asleep. And then they jump!—"

"Spider?" said Freddy. "What is spider?— Like peeg?" He got up. "Show me room."

"Sure," said Mr. Bismuth. "I'll take you up. Carl'll be glad to let you have it if you *want* it —ha, ha! But I guess you won't when you see it."

There really were spiders in Mr. and Mrs. Bean's old room, which had been taken over by Carl because his mother said he was delicate. And those spiders were old friends of Freddy's, a Mr. and Mrs. Webb. They usually lived in the house in the winter and the cow barn in the summer, but when the Bismuths had been at the Beans' for a while, a lot of flies heard about the cookie crumbs and jam that had got around on the furniture, and they sneaked down the chimney. They were pretty fresh, even for flies, and they buzzed around and lit on Mr. Bean's nose and fell in the milk and generally behaved very badly. So Mrs. Bean asked the Webbs to come back into the house. They had caught a lot of the flies and beaten them up, but there were still a good many, and it kept the spiders busy. "It's terrible hard work at our age," Mr. Webb said, "but there ain't anything we wouldn't do for Mrs. Bean. Ain't that so, mother?" And his wife said: "That's how it is, Webb."

When Freddy and Mr. Bismuth, followed by Mrs. Bismuth and the children, went up into Carl's room, Mr. Webb was having his after-breakfast nap on the back of a framed picture of Mr. and Mrs. Bean, taken on their wedding day, and Mrs. Webb was stalking a fly who had eaten too much chocolate cake and gone to sleep on the ceiling.

Mr. Bismuth pointed at her. "There's one of 'em. Terrible creature! One bite from those fangs and you begin to shake all over, and then you turn blue—Oh, excuse me," he said; "wouldn't work in your case, Captain, ha, ha!"

"Poison, eh?" said Freddy. "I kill 'em for you." He reached in a pocket and pulled out a little flashlight about as big as a pencil. "Death ray," he explained. "Kill fly, kill elephump. Very strong ray. Kill Bismut' too." He grinned and pointed it at Carl, who shrank back, squealing: "Pa! Make him quit!"

"There, there, my boy," said Mr. Bismuth. "He's just joking. Death ray, indeed! Ha, ha— why it's only a flashlight."

"You tink so?" said Freddy. "I show you. You see spider?" He pointed the flashlight at Mrs. Webb, waving it about to make her look down at him. For spiders as a rule don't pay any attention to people; they consider it a waste of time. People seldom talk about anything that would interest a spider, and as Mrs. Webb put it: "They're certainly not pretty to look at." And she would look admiringly at Mr. Webb, whom she considered very handsome and even rather dashing.

Although Mrs. Webb had been informed that Freddy was disguised as a Neptunian, she

He leveled the flashlight at them. . . .

was startled when she saw him. She abandoned her pursuit of the fly and ran quickly across to the picture frame to wake up her husband. After a minute they both came out on the ceiling and waited to see what Freddy wanted. They laughed until they were almost in hysterics when they saw him, but Freddy didn't know it, for spiders' laughter is on a small scale and unless you're within an inch of them you can't hear it at all. And of course their expressions are pretty dead pan.

They wanted to show him, though, that they recognized him, so they stood up on their last pair of legs and waved all the others at him. That was what he wanted to know. He leveled the flashlight at them and said: "O you spiders! Now I shoot you with death ray." Then he snapped on the flashlight.

"All right, mother; let's go!" said Mr. Webb. And the two spiders let go of the ceiling and dropped down on to the carpet. Spiders are so light that it doesn't hurt them to drop like that. Then Freddy went over and picked them up and they played dead while he showed them to the Bismuths.

"You like I turn ray on you?" he said, pointing the flashlight at them.

The two children and their mother began crying again, but Mr. Bismuth said in a shaky voice: "Well, sir, Captain; that was quite a demonstration, ha, ha; yes indeed! And of course now that the room is quite safe, I am sure that Carl will want to let you have it while you are here. Eh, my boy? you'll show the old hospitable Bismuth spirit, I'm sure." And when Carl opened his mouth to protest, Mr. Bismuth caught him a backhand swipe on the ear, and before he could recover: "That's my fine generous lad," said his father. "There you are, Captain. Room's yours as long as you want it."

Freddy dropped the spiders carefully into a small vase and tucked the flashlight back in his pocket. Then he grinned his ferocious grin. "I thank," he said. "Maybe not use death ray on boy today."

But by this time Mrs. Bismuth, weeping loudly, had hustled Carl and Bella out of the room.

CHAPTER
14

Freddy had a good deal of fun all the rest of the day. At dinner, when Mr. Bismuth tried to spear the last slice of meat off the platter before anybody else could reach it, Freddy rapped him over the knuckles with the flashlight and then pointed it at him; and Mr. Bismuth turned pale and said: "Thank you, I think I won't have any more." So Mr. Bean got the slice, which was the first one he had had.

After dinner Mr. Bean said: "Captain, I'm busy today, got to get that brook back in its old bed and see if I can save some of my garden. But maybe Mr. Bismuth will show you over the farm. Maybe you'd like to see how we handle things here on earth. Ed," he said, "be sure to show him the pig pen."

"Oh, why do you want to show him that dusty, cluttered up old place?" said Mrs. Bean.

"Show place," said Mr. Bean. "Homes of famous pigs. Typewriter on which deathless poems composed. Disguises worn by distinguished detective."

Mrs. Bean laughed. "Those disguises were probably the worst disguises ever put on. They never fooled anybody. Freddy was never a cowboy, he was a pig in a cowboy suit; he was never an old woman, he was just a pig in a bonnet and shawl."

"I wonder why she keeps trying to belittle me?" Freddy thought, as he went out with Mr.

Bismuth. "I thought she liked me better than that." It made him sort of unhappy.

As soon as he had Mr. Bismuth alone he began pumping him full of stories about the vast riches to be found on Neptune. Did Mr. Bismuth like diamonds and rubies and emeralds? They were so plentiful that Neptunian boys played marbles with them. Gold? There was a hill of solid gold right back of Captain Neptune's house. Pearls? The Neptunian oysters produced pearls six inches in diameter. The end of Mr. Bismuth's nose quivered with eagerness as he asked questions, and presently he said: "I would like to visit your beautiful country. A great honor, even for a Bismuth, ha, ha! to be the first man to set foot on that planet. Perhaps you would take me in your flying saucer."

Freddy nodded. "Maybe I take. Byemby. But if so you come, you no steal from my peoples, eh?"

"Steal!" Mr. Bismuth drew himself up. "No Bismuth would so lower himself as to steal." He delivered quite a speech about the honor of the Bismuths.

"Last night you steal," said Freddy. "Dig up

joolery, belong ducklings. I watch. I see. Where you hide him, hey?"

"You saw—?" Mr. Bismuth looked startled. "I don't know how you know about this, Captain. You must be a mind reader, ha, ha!—well, I was not stealing that stuff." And he went on to explain. He told about the jewelry, and said that Uncle Wesley had come to him in great distress. The duck had been afraid that when the pond was drained, the mud would crack, thus exposing the jewels, which would then be anybody's for the taking. Would Mr. Bismuth dig them up and help Uncle Wesley hide them in some safe place? Mr. Bismuth would and did. And Uncle Wesley took them and went away with them. Did Mr. Bismuth know where? No, he did not.

That was Mr. Bismuth's story. Freddy didn't believe it. He didn't think Uncle Wesley had been with Mr. Bismuth at all last night. But there was no way of proving it. And where was Uncle Wesley? None of the other animals could remember having seen him for several days.

Not all of the animals had been entrusted with the secret of Freddy's disguise. They were all, of course, devoted to the Beans, but some, who were not very bright, like Mrs. Wogus, and others who were pretty gossipy, like many of the birds and some of the rabbits, hadn't been told. It was a risky business, letting so many animals know who Captain Neptune really was, but Freddy had an idea that he was going to need a lot of help before he got through.

As he went around the farm with Mr. Bismuth, some of them managed to be always near by. It might be Mr. and Mrs. J. J. Pomeroy, the robins, swooping in slow circles overhead, or Bill, the goat, walking sedately behind them, but ready at a sign from Freddy to lower his head and butt Mr. Bismuth right over the fence. Freddy was a little nervous about Bill, who was inclined to act on impulse and be sorry later. But Bill behaved well, and pretty soon gave place to Robert, the collie, who caught up with them at the pig pen, and went inside after them.

While Mr. Bismuth was telling Captain Neptune about Freddy, Robert walked around sniffing at this and that, and looking under things and on top of things, as dogs do. But suddenly he gave a louder sniff. Mr. Bismuth didn't notice that it was any different, but Freddy did, and he turned to see that the collie was looking into the closet where all the disguises that he used in his detective work were hanging on a long pole. Robert didn't go into the closet, but he gave Freddy a hard look and jerked his head to show that there was something inside that was not in order. Then he wandered out of the pig pen and sat down on the grass.

Mr. Bismuth evidently hoped that he could talk Captain Neptune into taking him for a trip in the flying saucer, for he stuck tight to Freddy all the rest of the afternoon. Freddy got pretty sick of talking in the terrible broken English that he had decided Captain Neptune ought to use, but he had to keep it up. He had to concentrate on it so hard that he didn't get a chance to think up any kind of a plan. And when they went in to supper he still didn't have any idea of how he was to go about it to get rid of the Bismuths.

Just before supper however he had a word with Robert, who asked him if he'd had a chance to investigate his clothes closet. "Well," said the dog, "I didn't want to do anything about it myself. You know, your first report when you thought you were on Mars, spoke of a little two-legged Martian with big yellow shoes. Of course you weren't on Mars, and what it was you saw, and Charles tried to catch, we've none of us been able to figure out. Well anyhow, I'd sort of had those big yellow shoes on my mind, and—well, it was kind of dark in that closet, but when I saw what looked like yellow shoes, back in, just under the edge of all those clothes—"

"You *saw* yellow shoes?" Freddy exclaimed. "Was there anybody in them?"

"Golly, I don't know. Could have been, I suppose. They didn't move. But I only saw the lower part, and not very well at that. They were sort of between a couple pairs of other shoes. You got any yellow ones?"

Freddy said: "No. Come on, let's run up and look."

But there were no yellow shoes in the closet when they got up there.

"Guess there was someone in 'em all right," Freddy said. "Wish you'd grabbed him."

"Wish I had," said Robert. "But I thought you'd want to see—"

Freddy said: "Oh, sure. That was all right.

Well, keep your eyes open. I'm going in to supper."

Freddy kept his flashlight beside his plate during supper, lifting it occasionally to point it at any Bismuth who gobbled, slurped, took too large mouthfuls, or tried to get more than his or her share. The result was that the Beans had their first full meal in a week, and the Bismuth table manners were almost acceptable.

Carl was the only one who didn't seem very much afraid of the flashlight. After it had been pointed at him two or three times he said: "Aw, that old death ray—it's nothin' but a little old flashlight, I bet. Go on, shoot it at me, I dare you.—Ouch!" he yelled, for his father had kicked his shin under the table.

"There, there, my boy," said Mr. Bismuth; "don't tease the Captain. Though that's a fine courageous spirit you show. Eh, Captain? That's the Bismuth for you—fearless, intrepid, reckless. Did I ever tell you about old Hendrik van Bismuth, captured by the Indians at Oriskany? Laughed fit to kill while they was scalpin' him. 'Quit ticklin' me!' he says. They let him go, naturally. Half scalped. Mrs. van B., she sewed it on again when he got home."

But Carl went right on grinning every time he looked at the flashlight, so Freddy thought he'd better put in a little demonstration which he had arranged with Cousin Augustus.

The four mice lived in a cigar box under the stove. Their job was to tidy up the kitchen floor after meals, which they did by eating up crumbs and making a pile of any non-edible things which Mrs. Bean could sweep up easily in a dust pan. Freddy had arranged a signal by tapping on his chair rung; he gave it now, and the mice came out and lined up on the floor in front of the stove.

"You, boy!" Freddy said, pointing at Carl. "You tink dis deat' ray no good, hey? O K, I show." He pointed the flashlight at the mice and clicked it on, and all four of them fell over on their backs with their feet in the air.

Freddy got out of his chair and picked one up—it was Eeny—and brought him over to the table. "You see? He limp; he no wiggle." He held Eeny up by the tail, ignoring the dirty look that the mouse shot at him. Then he got the cigar box out and put the four mice in it and shoved it back under the stove. "You like I shoot you now?" he said to Carl.

And of course Carl began to cry, and then Bella began, and Mrs. Bismuth chimed in. But Mr. Bismuth quieted them down, and when he could be heard, he said: "You haven't got a spare one of those things, have you, Captain? I'd like to buy it if you have."

All this time Mrs. Bean hadn't said anything, although as Freddy well knew, she was very fond of the mice. She looked at him with an expression which he couldn't make out, and then she went and got the cigar box. "I think you knew that these mice were pets, Captain," she said. "And so I don't think you'd kill them. For you have a kind face, even if it is blue. I'm going to try to revive them." And she took the box into the other room.

After supper Freddy managed to get off by himself, and he went up to the pig pen. There were no yellow shoes in the disguise closet, nor any sign that anybody had been there. He sat down in his own big dusty chair and he thought: "My, it's nice to be home again! Guess I'll sit here a while quietly." But he hadn't been sitting there more than five minutes when through the window his eye caught a flicker of movement up along the fence. As usual, the

dirt and the wavy glass in the window pane dis-
torted whatever it was, so that it changed shape
as it went slowly along. But what didn't change
was the color of its feet, which were yellow.
"The yellow shoes!" Freddy exclaimed, and
dashed out of the door.

Sure enough, there was the little creature
with the black bathrobe and the yellow shoes,
walking up towards the pasture. "Hey, you!"
Freddy called. It didn't turn its head, but it
moved more quickly, waddled fast for a few
steps, then tried to duck under the lowest strand
of barbed wire to the other side of the fence.
And the covering or bathrobe or whatever it
was caught on the wire and was pulled off. And
under it was a white figure . . . "Uncle Wesley!" Freddy yelled. Of course; why hadn't he
figured it out; those yellow shoes were only the
duck's yellow webbed feet.

Uncle Wesley wasn't a fast runner. Freddy
caught him in a matter of seconds. He was good
and mad, too. "Oh, let me alone, can't you?"
he quacked. "I'm minding my own business,
and I will brook no interference from any offi-
cious upstart like you."

"Oh, pooh!" said Freddy. "You're going to

It was a white figure—Uncle Wesley.

brook plenty, Wes. You've got a lot of explaining to do. In the first place, how did you know me in this disguise?"

"You appear to think," said the duck, "that you are the only animal skilled in detective work on this farm. Let me tell you, sir, that if I turn my mind to it—"

"Oh, sure, sure," Freddy interrupted. "You've been trailing me some of the time. I can see that. But why are you hiding out? Not very kind to your nieces, is it, to let them think you've been murdered? And how about Bismuth? He's got the jewelry. Where has he hidden it?"

It took some time, and several threats, to get Uncle Wesley's story, but Freddy got it finally. After Mr. Bismuth had seen the duck's letter in the newspaper, complaining about the loss of mud from the pond, he had come to see him. They had had several consultations, and Mr. Bismuth had suggested changing the course of the brook. They disguised themselves, since Mr. Bismuth felt that Mr. Bean would not approve, and having scouted the stream, found a place where there was low ground on the west side of the Big Woods; at one spot there was just a little ridge between this and the stream bed. A trench dug through the ridge for a few yards would lead the water into a new bed, and would, so Mr. Bismuth said, form a new pond with the richest and most nutritious mud farther down.

"I didn't know that it would be led into the garden," Uncle Wesley said. "But of course once it was done, there was very little I could do about it."

It didn't occur to the duck at first to wonder why so selfish and dishonest a man as Mr. Bismuth would take so much trouble to help him. But then the questions that were asked about his nieces' jewelry made him suspicious. "I fancy," he said pompously, "that I am not without skill as a detective. I retained my disguise, which made me practically invisible—"

"Except for those big feet," remarked Freddy.

"The feet," said Uncle Wesley, "are not the feature by which one most readily recognizes an acquaintance. As perhaps you have learned."

"You've got me there," said the pig.

"There are methods of detection," said Uncle Wesley, "in which a simple uninstructed duck, like myself, who uses his brains, can teach even a professional, uh—private eye, I believe you call yourself."

"I don't," said Freddy. "Get on with your story."

"From the moment my suspicions were aroused," Uncle Wesley continued, "I shadowed—I believe that to be the correct term—Mr. Bismuth. I was close by when he dug the jewelry up. But in the excitement of your capture, and of his flight, I lost sight of him."

"You don't know then what he did with the stuff?" Freddy asked. "And did you ask him to dig them up, so you could hide them in a safer place?"

"No to both questions," said Uncle Wesley. "And now if you are finished with this entirely unauthorized cross-examination—"

"I'm not," Freddy cut in. "I want to know why you're slinking about with a piece of cloth over your head like somebody trying to haunt a house. Why don't you go home? I suppose you're afraid Mr. Bean will blame you for flooding his garden—"

Uncle Wesley flew into such a rage at this suggestion that Freddy was sure that it was

right. "I am not 'slinking,' as you call it!" he
quacked. "I have never, in my life, slunk! I am
watching every move that Bismuth makes; I am
searching for the hiding place of my nieces'
jewelry, and if it is 'slinking' to attempt to recover their property, then I do indeed 'slink.' "

"O K, O K," Freddy said. "I withdraw the
word. You don't slink. And I must say, I admire
your courage in tackling a crook like Bismuth.
But—well, look, Wes: if I respect your disguise,
you must respect mine. Are you sure that if
Bismuth catches you, you won't tell him who
I am?"

"Sir," said the duck, puffing out his chest,
"do you think for a moment that I would fear
such a low vulgar fellow as this Bismuth? Let
me tell you—"

"Let *me* tell it," said a deep voice in the tree
overhead. There was a soft flutter of big wings
and Old Whibley swooped down, seized the
duck in his claws and flew off with him.

Freddy heard the owl's voice: "I'll keep him
out of mischief for a while."

And then a feeble quacking which died away
in the northern sky.

CHAPTER
15

Freddy slept that night in the big bedroom
which had once been the Beans', and was now
Carl Bismuth's. He left the door open, and before he went to sleep the mice came up to see

him. He asked them what Mrs. Bean had done to revive them.

"Nothing," said Eek. "Just said: 'Get up out of that and don't be silly.' So we got up and ran back under the stove. Guess your big death ray act didn't fool her for a minute."

"H'm," said Freddy. "Well I guess—" He broke off as three rabbits came hopping through the door. "Hey!" he said. "How'd you get into the house?"

"Back door," said Rabbit No. 23. "Screen's propped open, and the door's ajar."

"We think maybe old Bismuth's sneaked out and left 'em open," said No. 16. "We thought we'd ask you if you wanted him followed."

"He's in bed," said Eeny. "We just looked. He's got a clothespin on his nose, and some arrangement of rubber bands. I've seen braces on teeth, but I never saw one on a nose before."

"Makes him snore terrible, that clothespin," said Quik. "Shook two pictures off the wall last night, and a pitcher of milk walked right off the table and went smash on the floor. Never even woke him. Good milk, too." He licked his whiskers.

"Funny about the door being open," Freddy said. "The Beans never leave it that way. Well, yes; I think you'd better keep an eye on Bismuth if he goes out. By the way, who's this?" he asked, pointing to the third rabbit, who was rather smaller than 23 and 16, but had much larger ears.

"My oldest boy," said 23. "No. 84½."

"A half?" Freddy inquired.

"Sure. He's one of the twins."

"What do you call the other one then?"

"Why, 84 and the other half, of course," said 23.

"Isn't that kind of a long name to call if you want him in a hurry?" Freddy asked. "How about 84a and 84b?"

"Well, in practice, we just call 'em 'other' and 'brother,'" said 23. "But I kind of like a and b. I'll speak to their mother about it."

"Why did you bring him?" Freddy asked. "He's never done any investigating for the firm."

"Speak up, brother," said 23. "Why did you come?"

"Well, sir," said 84½, "my father has been

one of your trusted operatives for many years, and I thought if—well sir, if you tried me out, and I proved worthy, maybe I could work with him."

The mice began to giggle.

"Wants to be a private eye," said Eeny.

"Private ear, is more like it," said Eek. "Bet there ain't a whisper on the farm that misses those flappers."

"All right, all right!" said 84½ angrily, "You want to pick on me, I'll pick right back. Want me to tell Freddy what you were whispering about him to your brother just before we came into the room?" He imitated Eek's squeaky little voice. " 'Now we'll see the great detective do his stuff! The big dope! Why, he couldn't detect a—' "

"Skip it!" said Freddy. "If you want to work for Frederick & Wiggins you've got to have better control over your temper than that. But I'll give you a chance. You can help your father on this case, and we'll see what he says about your work."

So then he told them all that he knew, and said: "What we want first of all is to find where he's hidden the jewelry, and the money from Mrs. McMinnickle."

They were discussing this when the Webbs came in. Only they came in along the ceiling instead of along the floor, like the mice. This is the best way to go from one room to another in the dark, if you can manage it, because you don't fall over things.

Of course Freddy didn't know they were there until they slid down a strand of web and landed on his head. Any other pig would have shaken his head and tried to throw them off, but Freddy knew at once who they were and, even though they tickled, he stayed still, and only said: "Hello, spiders. Don't stamp around any more than you have to."

He felt the tickle move from the top of his head over to his left cheek, and Mr. Webb's tiny voice said in his ear: "Good evening, Freddy. Well, we haven't anything to report. The Bismuths haven't said a word to each other about the jewels. Maybe Mr. Bismuth hasn't told his wife that he stole them. Probably afraid she'd ask to wear that string of pearls, and the Beans would want to know where it came from."

"I wouldn't mind having that string myself,"

said Mrs. Webb. "Though what I'd do with a necklace, without any neck to hang it on, I'm sure I don't know."

Mr. Webb said: "You'd better stick to flies, mother. Though to tell you the truth, Freddy, these flies today—they're not like they used to be when I was a young spider. They've got no more manners than a centipede. It used to be, you could make a sort of gentleman's agreement with them, they would stay out of the house in the summertime, and mother and I, when we caught any of the local flies, we'd let 'em go. Of course, unless we were terrible hungry. But generally, we just dined off those we weren't personally acquainted with.

"But my land, these flies—I don't know what kind of folks they come from, but they've certainly been badly brought up. Walk all over the dining-room table, and in and out of people's ears—and no respect even for a fly swatter. You ought to hear the language they use! And they're rough customers, too. They'll rassle you all over the web, and sometimes it takes both of us to handle a big one."

"The truth of the matter is, Freddy," Mrs. Webb said, "that we're getting too old for this kind of work. Maybe 'twouldn't be so bad if we could get a good night's sleep once in a while. But I haven't had one in I don't know when. It's this snoring."

"I suppose it must be sort of annoying," Freddy said.

"Annoying!" Mr. Webb exclaimed. "How'd you like to try to sleep through two thunderstorms, a cyclone and an earthquake? We have to tie ourselves into bed, and even then every time Bismuth snores it's as if we were playing snap the whip."

They were pretty upset, and Freddy did his best to calm them down. He was sorry, he said, but as he saw it, the whole future of the Bean farm was at stake, and they'd just have to carry on.

As he had thought, they were indignant that he should have suspected them of wanting to quit. "But as *we* see it, Freddy," Mr. Webb said, "the future of the Bean farm depends on getting rid of the Bismuths. And that's mostly your job. We don't say you aren't trying, but are you losing any sleep over it? *We* are."

At which Freddy flared up and said he was doing the best he could, and if anybody thought they could handle it more efficiently, they were welcome to try. Perhaps he wouldn't have been so indignant if he had really had a good plan. He could have told the Webbs about it, and they would have been satisfied. But not having any plan, he got mad.

The Webbs were smart spiders. They knew Freddy wasn't mad at them, but at himself for not having thought up a plan. So they apologized for being cross, and then he apologized for being cross, and there was a great exchange of politenesses.

The mice were getting bored, for they had only heard Freddy's side of the conversation, and they began to giggle and poke one another in the ribs, and at last Eeny said in an affected voice: "Oh, dearie me, dearie me, what very polite animals we all are, to be sure!" And Quik said: "Pawdon me, deah Cousin Augustus, but did I step on your tail?" And Cousin Augustus said: "Not at all, not at all! It's a pleasure. Jump up and down on it if you wish, deah cousin."

Freddy laughed, and said: "Well, there's nothing more we can do tonight. Keep your eyes open, all of you. We have got to find where Bismuth has hid the stuff. Because we can't

drive him away by keeping him awake for a
week, or by scaring him with ghosts, or by hir-
ing wasps to sting him, or any of the ways we've
used before."

Eek wanted to know why not, and Freddy
said: "He's Mrs. Bean's guest. She'd be ashamed
of us if she found out we drove away somebody
that she'd invited to stay."

"You mean you're just stuck with a guest, no
matter how they act?" Eeny demanded. "Boy,
I've issued my last invitation, then."

So then the mice and the spiders left, and
Freddy went to bed.

When he went down to breakfast he found
Mrs. Bean at the stove, and Mrs. Bismuth and
the two children gobbling pancakes as fast as
they came off the griddle, while Mr. Bean sat
in the rocking chair by the window, puffing his
pipe and taking an occasional sip from a cup
of black coffee. He liked cream in his coffee,
but Bella had emptied the entire pitcher over
her oatmeal. Mr. Bismuth had gone out without
his breakfast, Mr. Bean told him.

Freddy said heartily: "Goot mornink all peoples," and sat down next to Bella. "Is nice, the
utmeal?" he asked, and he picked up a spoon

and dipped into the little girl's bowl. "My, my, is goot!" he said, and he pulled her dish over to him and began spooning it into his mouth as fast as he could.

Mr. Bean took the pipe out of his mouth and doubled up in his chair and fizzed with laughter, but Bella let out a roar. "Ma! Ma! The big pig has taken my breakfast!"

At first Freddy was startled, thinking that she had seen through his disguise. But then he realized that she was just calling him a pig because she thought he was greedy. Any reference to pigs as lazy or dirty or greedy always made him mad; he had written a number of his excellent poems on that subject; so when she grabbed for the bowl, he slapped her hands away. "Is bad manners, snatchings," he said.

Well then Carl chimed in and Mrs. Bismuth got up and put her arms around Bella and said that if her honored pa was there, nobody would dare steal her food.

"My poor defenseless baby!" she sobbed. "My little hungry Bella!" And they all wept and howled.

Freddy dropped the spoon in the now empty bowl. "Is noisy, dot Bella," he remarked. "Why she got name Bella?" he asked Mrs. Bismuth. "On account maybe she bellers?" He laughed. "Ha, is goot! Is big choke, not? Where is honorable pop? I like tell him big choke."

Freddy had been wondering where Mr. Bismuth was. It wasn't like him to be absent when a meal was on the table. Mrs. Bean brought a plate of pancakes and set it in front of Freddy. Carl, though he was now crying and yelling so hard that he had his eyes shut, seemed to know it was there and made a grab for it. Freddy rapped him over the knuckles with a knife, then felt in his pocket for the flashlight.

The flashlight wasn't there. Was that, he wondered, what had waked him last night? Had someone sneaked into his room?

He got up, picked up the plate, and took it over the stove. "You eat," he said to Mrs. Bean. "I go find mister, tell him big choke."

There was no one around outside. He went into the stable, where Hank told him that Mr. Bismuth had come in earlier that morning. "He acted kinda funny," the horse said. "Though I dunno—he always acts funny, doesn't he? Hard to tell with him, is he actin' funny or just natural."

"He acted kind of funny," the horse said.

"Sure, sure," said Freddy impatiently. "But what did he *do?*"

"Oh, that," said the horse. "Why he pointed a little flashlight at me and kept clicking it on and off, and he mumbles something about spiders and mice, and then he—"

But Freddy didn't hear the rest. He ran out of the stable. He was halfway to the house when he heard Mr. Bismuth call to him, and he turned and went reluctantly back. "Got something of yours, my bold Captain," said Mr. Bismuth, and held out the flashlight. "Guess you mislaid it last night. Ha, ha; you certainly fooled me for a minute or two, and it ain't easy to fool a Bismuth—no, sir! Fooled me good with that death ray stuff and the mice and all. Funny thing, too; it's marked here—see?—patented nineteen something-or-other. Batteries are same as I buy here in Centerboro. Maybe the Busy Bee's got a branch store on Neptune, hey?" And he laughed heartily.

Freddy felt his tail coming uncurled, but he knew he had to put up a brave front.

"Is so," he agreed. "Some tings we buy when we making trips to America in flying saucer. De deat' ray part, we put it in byemby. We put—I try eggsplain—we put little ogglewop under batt'ry. I show." He started to take out the batteries.

"A little oggle—what?" said Mr. Bismuth.

"Ogglewop, ogglewop," said Freddy impatiently. "See! We put him under batt'ry, then we connex ogglewop wit' two himblatts—I sorry —these Neptunish words, no can say in English —we connex, like I say, then must push button same time touching littly fizzleplick, so deat' ray working. See?"

"No," said Mr. Bismuth. "You trying to kid me? There ain't any pollywogs or whatever you call 'em in there. Look, Cap—"

"Listen," Freddy interrupted. "No be stoopit. You listen—you learning. We got here ogglewop, no? O K, so we take like waglish wit' some tollypin ranklums, an' we dorfin a humblymamma—"

"Ah, phooey!" said Mr. Bismuth, turning away in disgust. "You're a fake, Mister, and I'm going to show you up. You and your pollywogs!" He shoved Freddy aside and started towards the house.

But Freddy stopped him. "Just a minute," he said, and said it in his regular voice.

Mr. Bismuth stopped dead. He stood for a moment motionless, then he turned. "What . . . what's that?" he said doubtfully.

"I'd better tell you," Freddy said, "since you've found out so much. I'm a police detective. I'd show you my badge, but it's inside this suit where I can't get at it. So it will be much better for everybody if you go right on believing that I'm a Neptunian."

Mr. Bismuth stared at him. "It's a good disguise," he said. "You look sort of—you'll pardon me—but that face isn't your own, is it?"

"Rubber mask," Freddy said. "Had it made specially for this job."

"Well, well," said Mr. Bismuth. "And who are you investigating, if I might ask?"

"Ah!" said Freddy mysteriously. "I'm not allowed to answer that. But I can tell you that the case I *came* to investigate is not the one I'm investigating now. See here, sir: I will put my cards on the table. I know you stole the ducks' jewelry. I know you hid it, and I have a good idea where you hid it. I have only to tell Mr. Bean, or the state troopers, what I know, and you, my friend, will be locked up in a little room with bars on the window."

"Nonsense!" said Mr. Bismuth. "You saw me dig up the jewelry. But I did it to help that What's-his-name,—Wesley. I didn't keep it."

"So you say," Freddy replied. "Did anyone see you give it to him? Can you produce Uncle Wesley, and have him back up your statement? My friend, you are on a spot."

"Ha, ha!" said Mr. Bismuth. "You think being on a spot worries a Bismuth? Sir, Bismuths are always on spots. They revel in spots. There's nothing you could prove. Let me tell you, sir—"

"Let *me* tell *you*," Freddy interrupted. "I say that I could tell Mr. Bean, but I do not say that I will. If you were to give me—h'm, there was a string of matching pearls, among other things, with a ruby clasp. If you were to detach that clasp, and slide it into my pocket tonight at supper—well, then I will agree to forget everything I know about you. And I will go back to investigating the case I came here to investigate."

Mr. Bismuth was thoughtful for a minute, and Freddy thought: "I guess I've got him." But then he laughed again. "Dear me," he said, "you make me almost wish I did have that stuff. Pearls, hey? My Ambrosia would look nice in 'em—make her very happy, which is always the aim of a Bismuth—make folks happy. But I guess it can't be done. You see, mister, I ain't got the jewelry."

"Very well," said Freddy. "Then watch yourself, Bismuth." And he turned and walked away.

CHAPTER
16

Although there had been a good deal of excitement about the flying saucer which had been seen to land in the Big Woods, most of the talk had been in the neighborhood. Even in Centerboro people dismissed the story with a shrug. "Just another of these stories," they said, and only a few even came out to try to see it. Mr. Dimsey, the editor of the Centerboro *Guardian,* had written a piece about it, and about Captain Neptune, who was visiting at the Bean farm, but even he thought it was all just a hoax, for Mr. Bean had refused to allow him to come out and interview the Captain. A few people did drive out and looked at the rocket from a distance, and one or two remarked that it looked a lot like the one in which Uncle Ben was exploring the solar system. But when they were told that all space ships had to be built on much the same plan, they didn't think any more about it.

The only visitors at the house were Mr. Margarine and the local farmers, and Freddy had had to talk to them. This he did with such a queer accent, and using such strange words, that they soon got tired of trying to make sense out of the nonsense that he fed them, and went away. They did what most people do when they can't understand anything—they pretended that the whole thing wasn't there.

Mrs. Bean had wanted Captain Neptune to

give a lecture in Centerboro. "It would be very interesting," she said, "to hear about the Neptunians—what they wear and what they eat and so on. And about your fishing trips." Freddy had made up quite a long story about how at home he was captain of a space ship on the regular run between Neptune and Mars. He also took parties of Neptunians on fishing trips in the Martian canals. But Mr. Bean said no, Captain just wanted to go around quietly for a while, seeing how people lived on earth, so that he could take back a report to his employers. "He thinks maybe they can start a regular service between earth and Neptune," Mr. Bean said. "Says eventually they're goin' to work up regular cruises around the solar system—like these South American cruises they have now, visitin' a day or two on each planet. Make a nice vacation for us, Mrs. B. maybe next summer."

"Very nice," said Mrs. Bean, and didn't say any more.

Freddy had hoped to scare off the Bismuths with his death ray, and when that failed and Mr. Bismuth had threatened to expose him as an impostor, he had hoped that by threatening in his turn, he could get the thief to take him into

partnership. When that too failed, a less per-
sistent detective might have given up. But
Freddy was sure that if he hung on long enough
and left nothing to chance, but kept a complete
twenty-four hour watch on Bismuth, chance itself would turn in his favor. And indeed it was
chance, or a piece of luck, that gave him in the
end the clue he needed.

In the meantime he was like a juggler who
has to keep half a dozen balls in the air at once.
One of them, or maybe several, was the crew of
the space ship. He talked with them two or
three times daily, and they were getting restless.

"You're having all the fun, pig," Jinx said.
"How long do you think we're going to stay up
here? Besides, Mrs. P."—he lowered his voice—
"is making up more poetry. Yours isn't so bad,
just puts people to sleep, but hers—golly! She
reads it to us. We can't take much more. Even
Uncle Ben breaks out into a cold sweat when
she says: 'Listen to this!'"

"I can't help it," Freddy said firmly. "You'll
just have to stand it. I give you my word, Jinx,
it will mean disaster for the Beans if you come
down. Give me one more day."

When he left Mr. Bismuth Freddy took off

all his false hair and his uncomfortable space
suit and washed the blue off his face. There was
no point in keeping it on any longer. He went
up past the now flooded garden. Alice and
Emma were sitting on the bank. They were
watching something, and he stopped and stared,
for out in the middle of the pool something was
plunging along, and smoke was puffing out of
it and sparks were flying, and there was a great
flailing of the water. Through the spray it
looked like a small model of a Mississippi steamboat, ploughing along under forced draught.

Freddy came closer, and then he saw that it
was Mr. Bean, pipe in mouth, swimming across
the new pool on his back. Mr. Bean saw him
at the same moment and stood up, for the water
was only four feet deep. He had on the old
fashioned striped bathing suit with pants that
reached below the knees, and sleeves that
reached below the elbows. "Good morning,
Captain," he said. "Just thought I'd take a dip,
water looked so nice. 'Tain't everybody that can
swim in his own vegetable garden."

"I'm not Captain any more," Freddy said.

And he told Mr. Bean of his talk with Mr.
Bismuth.

"Maybe it's best this way," Mr. Bean said. "You wa'n't getting anywheres, I guess." He looked across the pool at Alice and Emma, who had each put up a webbed foot to hide their smiles, and were tittering genteelly at the old bathing suit. "You ducks stop giggling at me," he said with mock severity, and when they just giggled louder, he splashed water at them. Then they giggled so delightedly that Alice choked and had to be slapped on the back.

"Yes, sir," said Mr. Bean, "I believe I'm going to keep this swimmin' pool. Handy to the house in hot weather, and what's the use of my raisin' vegetables anyway; the Bismuths only eat 'em right up." He came ashore and they talked for a while, then Freddy went on.

A little distance up the new stream John came trotting toward him. "Look, Freddy," said the fox; "you know that queer sort of walking toadstool I saw the other day, that I thought was some creature that had come in the flying saucer? Well, I've been wondering about it ever since, what it could be, and—golly, I just saw it again. Up here a ways. Come on, I'll show you."

Freddy had been puzzled about this creature too. They went up along the fence that sepa-

"You ducks stop giggling at me!"

rated the woods on the west from Mr. Margarine's property. From it a stone wall ran west,
and from behind the wall came voices. They
sneaked up quietly.

"Why, yes ma'am, it's lovely," a little anxious
voice was saying, "but I'm afraid my mother
will be wondering where I am. I guess I'd better—"

A second voice interrupted. "I guess you'd
better stay right here. I'll explain to your
mother if necessary. Now listen—I think this is
one you'll like:

"O goodness me! O goodness gracious!
How large the universe! How spacious!
How large it is I greatly fear
That you have no distinct idear.
It really quite surprises us
To find it is so enorm-u-ous.
It just goes on mile after mile;
To reach its end's impossibile.
And you could travel weeks and years
And never come out anywheers.
Because for all your haste and rushing
When you get there, there isn't nusshing
There isn't nusshing there at all,

And you feel pretty miseraball,
For though you holler bloody murder
You simply can't go any furder,
And if—"

"Oh, please excuse me," the other voice in-terrupted, "but I really must get back home. My mother—"

"I thought we'd settled about your mother," said the first voice. "Now listen:

And down on the United States
Shine all the stars and satellates.
Above the trees, above the house,
The stars they shine all tremulouse.
Like little lamps they brightly shine,
A-burning high grade kerosine.
Each star in all the constellations
Winkles and twinks. My goodness gracions!
My goodness me! How truly beauteous
They are! And kind of cuteous,
The way they hide behind the moon
So you can't see just what they're doon'."

"What's 'cuteous' mean?" asked the smaller voice.

"Don't pretend to be any more stupid than

you are," said the first voice severely. "You
know quite well what it means."

"Yes, ma'am," was the doubtful reply. "But
my mother says—well, she says I'm not very
bright, and so there's a lot of words you use I
don't understand. Like 'impossibile.' Is that
really the way to say it?"

"How else could you rhyme it with 'mile'?
That's what a good poet does—makes words
rhyme that haven't ever rhymed before. Land
of love, any fool can use the regular rhymes—
smile, style, file, bile. It's real poetry when you
get a new rhyme that there ain't anybody ever
thought of before."

The voices were just across the wall. John
whispered to Freddy. "Not bad, hey, those
poems? Guess you're running into a little competition. Who is it?"

"Mrs. Peppercorn," Freddy said. "Darn it,
she's supposed to stay in the rocket; she hadn't
ought to be down here. Come on." And he
climbed up on the wall.

John hopped up after him—then, catching
sight of Mrs. Peppercorn, sitting there with her
umbrella over her head to keep the sun off, he
yelled in a frightened voice: "The Neptun-

ian!" and hopped down again and ran off. For of course it was the old lady in her space suit, with her umbrella up, whom he had seen the other day and taken for one of those who had landed here in the flying saucer. And beside her was a young chipmunk who, when she took her eye off him, saw his chance and scuttled away.

"Well!" she said indignantly when she saw Freddy. "How long do you intend to keep this foolishness up, young man? It's just as I thought —this whole affair is nothing but a practical joke of some kind. And in very poor taste, let me tell you. Instead of taking me to Mars, after I'd paid for my ticket and gone to considerable trouble and expense to prepare for the journey, all your fine Uncle Ben has done is jump this rocket thing a mile or so up into the Big Woods. We've never left the surface of the earth!"

"Oh, yes we did," said Freddy, and tried to explain what had happened. But Mrs. Peppercorn didn't listen. She put her umbrella down and shook it at him. "Don't you talk to me! You and your precious Uncle Ben! I should think you'd be ashamed of yourselves!" She went on at some length.

Freddy didn't see that he would gain anything by arguing. And now that Mr. Bismuth knew that he wasn't Captain Neptune, her wandering away from the ship didn't make much difference. He said: "Excuse me," and went on into the woods.

Old Whibley's tree had escaped the fire; Freddy went and knocked on the trunk, and presently the owl's deep voice said: "Good heavens, can't I get a little peace? What is it *now?*" He came out of his hole and looked down at the pig. "For anybody that's been to school and had all your advantages," he said, "you certainly do manage to come out in the darnedest costumes. What are you disguised as today?"

Freddy of course wasn't disguised at all now. But before he could think of any good answer, the owl said: "No, no; don't tell me. Let me guess." He put a claw to his beak. "Let me think; let me think! Though, dear me, it's pretty hard to think with that idiotic face gaping at me. Whoever made that mask was a genius; it has the most empty, brainless expression I've ever seen. Are you Simple Simon today? Or—that little Bismuth boy? Or—"

"Oh, cut out the funny stuff," Freddy said crossly. "I thought you wanted to help Mr.

Bean, but if you're just going to be comical—"

"Why it's Freddy!" Whibley exclaimed. "Of course, how stupid of me! I beg your pardon, Freddy; it's so long since I'd seen you that I'd sort of forgotten how much you look like something that nobody has ever seen before except in dreams. Not very pleasant dreams, either. Well now, what can I do for you?"

It was no good getting mad at the owl; he would always have the last word. Freddy said: "I haven't got my walkie-talkie, and I thought maybe you'd go up and tell Uncle Ben and Jinx and Georgie they can come down now. And I want to know if Charles and Uncle Wesley are here. You could let them go now."

"Glad to," said the owl. "Glad to. They're no addition to a quiet home. Argue, argue, argue—from morning to night. Listen!" And from the hole in the tree Freddy could hear voices. Apparently they were arguing about their appearance.

"An elegant appearance, my dear sir," Uncle Wesley was saying, "is naturally what I have aimed at, and I fancy that I have acquired it. Though of course dignity and—ah, a certain graciousness of manner are natural to me. I cannot feel but that the red hat you wear is slightly on the—let us not say *vulgar*—but rather on the juvenile side."

"My good duck," Charles replied, "that is not a hat, it is a comb, it's part of me. And I see no harm in a touch of color. Look at my tail-feathers. They have been greatly admired, let me tell you. For my money, that little spike you call a tail is strictly for laughs. Waggle, waggle; and then down you go under water and stick it straight up in the air. Ha!"

"Indeed!" said Uncle Wesley huffily. "Well, I'd rather be finished off with a neat white spike than with a ratty looking old feather duster."

"Don't you 'indeed' me," Charles retorted. "Maybe you don't like the looks of my tail, though better people than you have considered it very handsome and dashing. I don't have a bow-legged waddle, either. I walk along gracefully, my wife following three steps behind, as is seemly . . ."

Whibley gave his hooting laugh. "How Henrietta would enjoy that, eh, Freddy? I can just hear her."

"Does she know he's here?" Freddy asked.

"Yes, I told her. She said keep him as long as

I liked: it was nice and peaceful in the hen-house. But I suppose now I'll have to let him go."

A robin flew down and lit on the ground in front of the pig. "Say, Freddy," he said, "Mr. Webb wants to see you. Better hurry up—he says it's important."

Whibley said: "Go along, pig. I'll go up to the space ship and tell 'em. Wait a minute—you can take this with you." He went into his nest and there was a scrabbling and a squawking, and a feather or two floated down. And then Charles came tumbling out. He got his wings spread before he was halfway to the earth, but like all roosters he was a clumsy flier, and he hit the ground with a bump.

He shook his feathers angrily into place. "I fail to see the need for all this rough stuff," he said. "After all I was a guest in Whibley's home; when you say goodbye to a guest you don't usually kick him downstairs.

"However," he said, "I'm glad to be out of the place. Whibley's all right. If you care for owls—I can't say I do. But that Wesley! Golly!" He continued to complain about the duck all the way back to the farm.

CHAPTER
17

Mr. Webb was waiting for Freddy up in the bedroom. He dropped down on the pig's nose and walked up to where he could shout in his ear. "We caught a fly a while ago, Freddy," he said, "and I think you ought to hear what he has to say." He shinned back up his rope and then he and Mrs. Webb lowered the fly down on to Freddy's nose. The captive had the use of his legs, but his wings were tied so that he couldn't escape.

"Just tell the detective what you have told me," said Mr. Webb. "There's no need to be frightened; we'll let you go if you'll do as we want you to."

"Well, sir," said the fly, "you know that heap of stones up in the corner of the lower pasture? I've got an aunt that lives up near there, and she'd found a lot of crumbs—fruit cake crumbs, and fresh ones—around that rock pile."

"Fruit cake?" said Freddy. "What would they be doing up there? Did your aunt know who dropped them?"

"No, sir," said the fly. "She was kind of puzzled how they got there because she knew about fruit cake, but she hadn't seen any in a long time—not since my grandfather brought her a piece from that Miss McSomebody who lives down the road."

"McMinnickle," said Freddy. "Yes, she's the only one that makes fruit cake that I know of.

But she wouldn't be eating it up in our pasture. Where is your aunt?"

"Yes, where is she?" said the fly angrily. "Ask these spiders. I told her about the good rich crumbs these Bismuths strew all over the Bean house, and she came down with me. She was a good kind soul—never harmed anybody, and never suspected that anybody would harm her. She was sitting on the edge of a glass of water on the bedside table, eating a piece of cheese—goodness sakes, it was only a crumb; nobody ought to grudge her a little piece like that! And these big brutes jumped her. Pushed her into the glass and she drowned." The fly sniffed, and wiped a tiny tear from his left eye with one foot.

"Dear, dear," said Freddy, "very sad end, indeed. Webb, how could you?"

The spider winked at his wife. "Can't understand it," he said. "Don't know what came over me. Mother, you should have stopped me."

"No doubt," said Mrs. Webb. "I'll try it next time you're stalking a fly. Well, Freddy, you see we caught this fellow here, and he was so sticky we almost let him go. All messed up with that fruit cake. I must say, most of these flies aren't very neat eaters."

"Freddy doesn't care about that, mother," Mr. Webb said.

"No. Well, anyhow, we were curious, and so we asked some questions, and when he told us about the fruit cake, we thought we'd better tell you."

Freddy said: "I'm glad you did. Mr. Bismuth has been down to see Miss McMinnickle several times. He likes the fruit cake she gives him. So I guess we'd better go up and look over that rock pile. 'Tisn't a comfortable place to sit, so we can be sure he didn't just take a piece of cake up there to eat it. He must have done more than that. Let your prisoner go—we'll just run up and see."

It was plain that the rock pile had been disturbed within the last few days. Freddy turned over a stone under which the pressed-down grass was still green, and a small beetle scuttled off. But Mr. Webb jumped down and gave chase, and presently cornered the fugitive against a big flat rock. Freddy could see that they were talking; the beetle, at first rather scared, became presently much excited and waved his feelers and pointed with his forelegs. After a minute Mr. Webb let him go, and came back to Freddy.

"Funny," he said; "I can't make it out. That fellow lives down underneath these rocks, and he says somebody did tumble them all around the other night. But he says that there's a hole down underneath the pile, and some kind of a big ferocious bug has moved in there. He says when he peeks in at it he can see it glaring at him with one bright red eye."

"A bright red eye," said Freddy thoughtfully. "That necklace of Alice and Emma's had a ruby clasp. H'm, guess we'd better dig that ferocious bug out." And he began hastily throwing aside the rocks.

And sure enough, there in the hole underneath the stones was the pearl necklace with the ruby clasp, and a heap of rings and chains and brooches.

The Webbs were so delighted that they stood up on their last pair of legs and danced a little dance on Freddy's nose—until it tickled so unbearably that he made them stop. "Don't fly off the handle," he said. "This is a piece of good luck, but Bismuth isn't in jail yet." He piled the rocks back, and then hurried down to the house.

Mrs. Bean was out on the back porch. "Well,

The Webbs were so delighted.

Freddy," she said, "you're home again. How'd you leave all the folks on Mars?" And then when he looked embarrassed and began to stammer something: "Now, now," she said consolingly, "you didn't suppose you could fool me as easily as all that, did you? That was a good disguise all right, but I'd know your voice anywhere. And when Captain Neptune made the same little squeal that you do when he got excited—well, I was sure."

"You mean you knew we never got to Mars?" Freddy asked.

"Of course. If Cousin Augustus had gone in the space ship, that would have left only three of the mice here. "When I saw four, I knew you'd either got back, or else had never gone."

Although Freddy had located the money and the jewelry, he still hadn't proved that Mr. Bismuth had hidden it. So first he had a conference with Mr. Bean, who called up the state troopers, and then he hunted up Mr. Bismuth. "Look, Mr. Bismuth," he said, "I know what's under that rock pile in the corner of the pasture. But those ducks aren't any special friends of mine, and—well, what's it worth to you to have me keep my mouth shut?"

Mr. Bismuth turned pale, but at first he tried to bluff. "Rock pile?" he said. "I don't know any rock pile. What are you talking about?"

So Freddy told him. Even then he wouldn't admit that he had had anything to do with hiding the stuff. "But," he said, "I see no reason why we should embarrass everybody by digging the stuff up. Money is the root of all evil, they say; and roots should remain decently buried, eh? And after all, ha, ha—what good is jewelry to ducks? No, no, my boy; take a Bismuth's word for it: better leave the stuff right where it is."

He talked for quite a while, and Freddy appeared to be partly convinced, and said—well, he'd think it over.

But that night the troopers, who were lying in wait behind the stone wall, arrested Mr. Bismuth as he was coming down from the pasture with the jewelry in his pocket. They took him down to the jail in Centerboro, and the sheriff locked him up.

During the next week, while Mr. Bismuth was awaiting trial, a great many people came up to the Big Woods to have a look at the space ship. As soon as Uncle Ben and Jinx and Georgie came home, and it was understood that they had really been whizzing around in outer space, even though they hadn't got to Mars, there was great excitement all over the country. All the big papers sent reporters to interview them, and offers for lectures and public appearances on television showered upon them.

Uncle Ben would have been glad to accept some of these offers, in order to make enough money to buy fuel for another attempt to reach Mars, but of course a man who only talks in sentences two words long isn't much good on a stage. Freddy was too busy catching up on work in his detective business, and in his newspaper and the bank, to do anything, and Jinx also refused. "No sir," he said; "you don't get me up on any platform. Once you start that business you get like Charles—you just can't stop talking. Me, I'm a doer, not a talker." And when they asked him what it was he did, he said: "Sleep, mostly."

But Charles and Georgie both lectured, although after Georgie's second appearance he gave it up. He got so excited at the applause that he forgot to talk and just barked at the audience, and they laughed at him and hurt his feelings. But Charles was put under contract by one of the big lecture bureaus, and for the next year was hardly ever seen at the farm at all. He traveled all over the country, mostly by plane, with a secretary and a valet whose job it was to keep his space suit brushed and pressed; and one night he would speak in Buffalo and the next in Cleveland, and so on. It was the first time in his life that he had been able to talk as much as he wanted to. He made a lot of money, too, and most of it he turned back to Uncle Ben to be used in financing the next trip. I think it was pretty generous of him.

Mrs. Peppercorn also lectured. She wore her space suit and carried her umbrella, and she would have been fully as successful as Charles, but each time when she was about halfway through her lecture she would begin to talk about her poetry. And then she would recite some of it. "So out we flew to the wild blue yonder, only 'tain't blue, it's black as thonder." So it began. And first the people in the back row would get up and tiptoe out, and then the next few rows would leave, not so quietly. Along about then she would notice what was going on, and she would get mad. "Now, you folks, you

down in front here anyway, you set right still!
Ain't you got any manners? Now here's another
poem." But before she got through the first
verse the rest of the audience would have risen
as one man and stampeded from the hall.

The only person or animal who ever listened
with interest, or even with patience, to Mrs.
Peppercorn's poetry, was Mrs. Wiggins. The
cow was still in jail, and was to be tried on the
same day as Mr. Bismuth. She hadn't minded
being locked up, for the Centerboro jail was
known throughout New York State as being a
very happy jail; many criminals considered a
stay there as a delightful vacation, and they had
to be pushed out when they had served their
sentences. Mrs. Wiggins enjoyed it all, and
when Mrs. Peppercorn lectured to the prisoners, she was the only one left in the hall at the
end of the evening. After that they got quite
chummy, and Mrs. Wiggins began writing
poetry herself. It was even more terrible than
Mrs. Peppercorn's.

And at last came the day of the trial.

CHAPTER
18

Although it was raining heavily on the day of
the trials, the courtroom was packed to the
doors. There were as many people as animals
in the audience. For not only did Mrs. Wiggins

have many friends in Centerboro who were certain that she had never stolen the purse, but all of Freddy's friends—and their names, as the Centerboro Guardian put it, were legion—had come to hear him conduct the prosecution in the Bismuth case. Mr. Bismuth had no lawyer; he said he guessed a Bismuth could take care of his own defence, particularly, ha, ha, when he wasn't guilty. In the case of the State vs. Wiggins, a Mr. Herbert Garble was the prosecuting attorney. Defending Mrs. Wiggins was a formidable team of legal talent, headed by Old Whibley, with John, the fox, and Uncle Solomon, the screech owl, as assistants.

Mr. Bismuth had demanded a jury trial. Mrs. Wiggins said she didn't care, they could try her with a jury, or a judge, or they could just turn her loose and save a lot of trouble and expense. But everyone is entitled to a trial by jury if he wants it, so she said at last that as long as she was going to have a trial, she might as well have one with all the fixin's. She and Mrs. Peppercorn, who visited her every day in the jail, made up verses about it.

"I don't have to worry," she said, "so bring on your jurry."

The first hour was devoted to the selection of twelve jurors who would serve on both cases. It is perhaps of interest to list their names. There were six men: Mr. Beller and Mr. Rohr from the music store, Dr. Wintersip, Mr. Metacarpus, the manager of the Busy Bee, Mr. Hinkelbaugh, the butcher, and a young farmer whose name nobody could either spell or pronounce. And there were six animals: Ronald, Charles' son-in-law, Theodore, the frog, Mac, the wildcat from up in the woods, Peter, the bear, Jerry, Mr. Witherspoon's horse, and Jinx, who was foreman of the jury.

The McMinnickle case came first. Miss McMinnickle gave her testimony, and then a state trooper testified that he had found her empty pocketbook in the cow barn. Mr. Bismuth was called as a witness, and he told of the tea party at Miss McMinnickle's house. Yes, he had seen the pocketbook; it was on the mantelpiece, just under a picture of an old gentleman with long whiskers and a squint.

"He has *not* got a squint!" said Miss McMinnickle angrily. "That is my grandfather and he had very beautiful kind brown eyes, and they were not—"

Bang! went Judge Willey's gavel. "Your grandfather's appearance is immaterial, irrelevant, and has nothing to do with the case. He could have been crosseyed and had warts, and it would still have nothing to do with the guilt or innocence of the prisoner. Kindly refrain from further comment, madam."

But Miss McMinnickle's dander was up. "I'll comment if I feel like it," she said. "I'm certainly not going to sit here and hear people make fun of my grandfather."

"Nobody's making fun of him," said the judge. "He was an estimable gentleman. I knew him well, and you are wrong about the squint. He did have one, though it was a slight one and only noticeable in a bright light."

"Your Honor," said Old Whibley, "will you kindly set me straight on a minor point? I am a trifle confused whether Mrs. Wiggins or Miss McMinnickle's grandfather is the defendant in this case. As attorney for the defence, am I trying to clear Mrs. Wiggins of the charge of theft, or Miss McMinnickle's grandfather of the charge of squinting? I shall be grateful for light on this point."

"I think we have all strayed a little from the

argument," said Judge Willey. "Mr. Garble will resume the examination of the witness." So Mr. Bismuth went on with his testimony. And now he made a statement which was very damaging indeed to Mrs. Wiggins. He said that as they were leaving Miss McMinnickle's house, he saw Mrs. Wiggins reach up and take the pocketbook from the mantelpiece when her hostess was not looking.

Then Mr. Garble sat down and Old Whibley flew over and perched on the corner of the witness box and started his cross-examination.

"Mr. Bismuth," he said, "kindly cast your mind back to the afternoon in question, when you took tea with Miss McMinnickle. You stated, I believe, that you saw the pocketbook on the mantelpiece."

"I did," said Mr. Bismuth.

"You said that it was a square brown pocketbook, somewhat worn at the edges?"

"Yes, sir."

"And that it had a brass clasp?"

"Yes."

"And was lined inside with red leather?"

"No, sir; the lining was brown clo—" Mr. Bismuth stopped short. "At least it was my impression that it was lined with brown cloth. That would be the most likely lining for such a pocketbook, would it not? Of course, it may have been red. Since I did not see the lining—"

"You can't have it both ways," said the owl testily. "Either it was red or brown. Take your choice—which was it?"

But Mr. Bismuth had recovered himself. "I am sorry; I don't know. Even a Bismuth—ha-ha! —can't see the inside of a closed pocketbook."

"You did not open the pocketbook, then?"

"What do you mean—'then'?" Mr. Bismuth demanded. "Not then or at any other time."

"Quite so," said Whibley. "Then of course you did not notice that it contained the one hundred and eighty-three dollars which Miss McMinnickle claims was stolen."

"A *hundred* and eighty-three!" Mr. Bismuth exclaimed. "There wasn't any hundred and eighty-three; there was only—" He stopped again, and Mrs. Bismuth, who was sitting in the front row, crying quietly, said in a horrified voice: "Oh, pa! Oh, be careful!"

"Now Mr. Bismuth," said Whibley, "you stated, I believe, that you saw Mrs. Wiggins

"Are you aware, sir, that a cow has hoofs?"

reach up and take the pocketbook from the
mantel as you were leaving. Is that correct?"

"It is."

"Now think carefully. Which hand did she
take it with?"

Mr. Bismuth said confidently, and without
hesitating a moment: "The right hand."

"Quite so," said the owl. "You would say
that she grasped it firmly with her fingers,
would you not?"

"Yes, sir. I—" He stopped abruptly. Mrs. Bismuth was trying frantically to attract his attention, shaking her head and putting a finger to
her lips. He stared at her for a second, but before he could say anything, Whibley pounced.

"Will you kindly explain to the jury how a
cow could grasp anything with her fingers? Are
you aware, sir, that a cow has hoofs?"

"Yes," Mr. Bismuth stammered. "I misspoke
myself. It was the impression I got, seeing her
reach for the pocketbook, and—"

Whibley's deep voice interrupted him. "I
suggest, Bismuth," he said, "that you did indeed see fingers seize the pocketbook. But they
were not the non-existent fingers of a cow. They
were your own thieving fingers! I suggest," the

owl said, "that in order to escape the due penalty for your crime, you are attempting to throw the blame on my client, an upright and honest cow, against whom not the faintest breath of suspicion has ever blown. A truly dastardly act!"

"Oh, pa!" Mrs. Bismuth wailed. "Oh, children, your honored pa is sunk!" And all the Bismuths burst into loud sobs and had to be led from the courtroom.

Then Old Whibley addressed the jury. He spoke shortly and to the point. Mr. Bismuth had plainly lied, he said, in order to throw the blame on Mrs. Wiggins. He asked for a verdict of not guilty. The jury filed out, and in five minutes came back. The verdict was "Not guilty."

Then the jury rose and gave Mrs. Wiggins three cheers, and the audience in the courtroom threw up hats and pounded one another on the back and yelled. For Mrs. Wiggins was indeed popular in Centerboro. And Judge Willey just looked down at them and smiled and didn't bang his gavel once.

Outside, on the courthouse steps, Mrs. Wiggins paused, for a large crowd had gathered to cheer her; and there were cries of: "Speech! Speech!"

"Land sakes, I can't make a speech," she said. "Tell you what: I'll recite a poem I composed while in jail." And she began.

"Although in jail in Centerboro,
I do not fret or stew or worro.

And confidently I confront
The judge, because I'm innosunt.

Tho I'm a cow, I am no coward
I have not flinched when thunder rowered.

When lightning flashed I've merely giggled
Like one whose funnybone is tiggled.

And I shall never give up hoping
That soon the jail front door will oping

And I'll once more enjoy my freedom
On Bean's green fields. When last I seed 'em

They were a fair and lovely vision
And so for my return I'm wishun.

I hope that Bismuth will get his'n
And spend a good long time in prison."

The cheering which had greeted the first verses became louder, and as she tried to go on it was almost continuous, drowning her out completely. She hesitated for a minute or two, then realizing the impossibility of being heard, went back into the courthouse.

Jinx dug Freddy in the ribs. "That's a poke in the eye for old mother Peppercorn, eh? Her only poetry pupil, and the crowd just stands there and yells so it won't have to hear the stuff."

Freddy said with a grin: "I understand the Centerboro Rotary
Has asked her to come and talk about po'tery."

"Yeah," said the cat. "Well, don't let it get your goatery."

CHAPTER
19

The trial of the State vs. Ed Bismuth opened
with Alice and Emma on the witness stand. In
their flat quacking voices they told about their
jewelry, how it was hidden in the pond, and
how when the pond went dry they worried that

it might be stolen. The jewels were held up and a long "Ah!" of admiration and wonder went through the audience as the flashing brilliance of precious gems lit the gloomy courtroom. Then Freddy told how he had seen Mr. Bismuth digging in the pond, and of the information given by the fly which had led to the rock pile and the digging up of the jewels. After which the trooper told of capturing Mr. Bismuth and finding the jewels in his pocket.

Then Freddy called Uncle Wesley. But before the duck could take the stand Mr. Bismuth jumped up. "I object, your Honor," he said. "I object to the entire conduct of this trial. I submit that not only the entire jury, but the judge himself—all are friends of Mrs. Wiggins, and all are hostile to me. I submit that they have prejudged this case and even before the evidence is heard, have convicted me. I demand a fair trial."

Judge Willey looked down at him over his glasses. "There is a certain amount of truth in what you say," he said. "But unless we go outside of this state, I do not know where we can pick a jury which will not be hostile to you. It is well known that you pocketed money gained from the sale of tickets to Mars in a—"

"I object," shouted Mr. Bismuth. "I am being tried for the theft of these jewels. You have no right to bring that up."

"You are correct," said the judge. "Objection sustained. I withdraw that remark and direct that it be stricken from the record. However, you have impugned the honor of this court. You have stated that I have prejudged the case, have implied that you will not get a fair trial here. If that isn't contempt of court I'll eat my gavel. And it will cost you fifty dollars, Mr. Bismuth."

"Your Honor has misunderstood me," Mr. Bismuth said. "I beg that you will reconsider. Such a charge as you suggest that I have made against you is so far beyond the bounds of credibility that it is laughable. Your probity and uprightness are unquestioned—are as well known as—ha, ha, I was going to say: as that of a Bismuth. But in Centerboro—"

He was interrupted by a deep laugh from Old Whibley.

Judge Willey banged with his gavel. "I will *not* have hooting in this courtroom, counsellor. Is that clear?"

"Quite, your Honor," said the owl. "But I

wasn't hooting; I was just laughing at this Bismuth's telling us how honest he is. Try it for laughs yourself, judge; I think you'll get a giggle out of it."

"That will do," said the judge. "You are trying to prejudice the judge and jury against the defendant, and goodness knows we're prejudiced enough already, without any help from you."

At this, Uncle Solomon laughed. It was the loud rippling mirthless laugh of the screech owl, and Judge Willey glared down at him. "This court seems to be plagued by owls this morning," he said. "You of all people, Uncle Solomon, should respect the solemnity of the court, even if you do not respect the dignity of the magistrate who happens to be presiding."

"A correction, your Honor," said Uncle Solomon in his precise voice. "May I say that I respect the dignity of the magistrate, this particular magistrate, very profoundly." Judge Willey bowed, and could not prevent a slight smirk from passing across his face. "But," the screech owl went on, "I do not see why solemnity is so desirable in this court. I do not see why good healthy laughter is incompatible with justice.

Personally, sir, I feel that one good laugh is worth seventeen scholarly Supreme Court decisions."

"Why there, sir, you find me in complete accord," the judge began.

But Freddy interrupted. "If it please the court, time is getting short and I would like to continue the examination of the witnesses."

"Of course, of course," said Judge Willey hastily. "Call the next witness."

So Uncle Wesley waddled up to the witness stand.

"Now, Uncle Wesley," Freddy said, "you first met the prisoner, I believe, when he came to see you about the mud in the duck pond. Is that correct?"

"Quite correct," said the duck. "My letter in the Bean Home News called attention to the loss of mud in the pond, mud on which our livelihood depends. Mr. Bismuth was good enough to comment favorably on the style of the writing, and the skill with which I had presented my case. He said—"

"The witness will confine himself to answering the questions. It is not necessary for him to repeat any compliments which the prisoner may

"Well, now, Uncle Wesley," Freddy said.

have paid him. We are not here to listen to his praises."

"Yet I would like to put these compliments in evidence," said Freddy, "for beside them I would like to put this letter." And he handed the judge the brown paper bag on which Uncle Wesley had written his complaint with a hard pencil. "I submit, your Honor, that nobody could honestly compliment the writer on such a scrawl."

The judge squinted at the bag, turned it upside down and then sideways, and then sniffed and handed it over to the foreman of the jury. "Quite true," he said. "But what do you intend to show by putting it in evidence?"

"Why, to show that the prisoner is dishonest."

"Well, we knew that anyway," said the judge. "Get on with your case."

"Well now, Uncle Wesley," Freddy said, "I believe that Mr. Bismuth changed the course of the stream that fed the duck pond, so that it ran in another bed and left the pond dry. Is that so?"

"Yes, sir."

"You saw him do this?"

"I was with him, sir. But I did not realize that

the water would flood out Mr. Bean's garden, or I would have refused to permit it."

"What you did realize, however, when the water was gone, was that your nieces' jewels would be plainly visible. Is that not so?"

Uncle Wesley now showed his first signs of hesitation. He said: "Why, I—er, yes I suppose so."

"And you then realized too, did you not, that there was danger that Mr. Bismuth, to whom you had talked about the jewels, might try to steal them?"

"There was danger that anyone might try to steal them," said the duck. He glanced at Mr. Bismuth doubtfully. Mr. Bismuth was not looking at him; but although the man's eyes were staring with ferocity off into space, his nose was pointed straight at the duck. It gave him an extraordinarily sinister and menacing expression. Uncle Wesley shivered slightly. "I naturally did not fear Mr. Bismuth nearly as much as some other characters I could mention—yes, some who are right in this courtroom!" he said, glaring at Freddy. "For I had taken Mr. Bismuth into my confidence about the jewelry; he had agreed to dig it up and conceal it in a safe place, so that it could later be turned over to its rightful owners, my nieces." Again he glanced fearfully at Mr. Bismuth, who nodded his head slightly as if satisfied with this speech. But he didn't turn his eyes towards the duck.

Freddy was completely taken aback by Wesley's statement, which was directly the opposite of what the duck had told him. He had expected to prove that Wesley knew nothing of the hiding of the jewels in the rock pile, and thus prove Mr. Bismuth guilty beyond the shadow of a doubt. But he said quickly:

"Wesley, you are lying. I will remind you that perjury is a very serious crime, and I will ask you straight: was it with your consent that Mr. Bismuth took those jewels?"

Uncle Wesley was agitated. He shifted from side to side on his big yellow feet and glanced sideways at the judge, and then at Mr. Bismuth. The judge didn't say anything, but Mr. Bismuth cleared his throat in what was almost a growl. And after a few preliminary quacks to get his voice under control, Wesley said: "Yes sir, it was."

"I see," Freddy said. "Then the story you told me, and told Old Whibley, about shadowing Bismuth, and watching him dig up the jewels, and then trying to find where he had hidden them, was all a lie? I put it to you that it was the truth, but that Mr. Bismuth has threatened you, and you are now afraid to offend him. You would rather let your nieces lose all the treasures, all the property they have in the world, than stand up and tell the truth. You would rather cringe before a cheap crook than stand up and do your duty like a true duck."

Uncle Wesley flew into a rage. "What I tell a brutal, treacherous owl, who kidnaped me and confined me in a dark and stuffy prison, is one thing. What I tell an old gossip of a pig who is always poking his nose into other people's business, is one thing. But what I now tell this jury is another thing, and it is the truth. Mr. Bismuth has my complete confidence. I asked him to take and keep the jewels. And has he not been true to his trust? Here are the jewels to prove it."

"Which the police took from him when he was running away with them," said Judge Willey. "You—Wesley—you are either a liar and a traitor, or a singularly stupid duck—I can't make out which. And I'm not going to try.

However, the jury will now go and consider their verdict. Though I do not see, in view of the testimony which has been given—I do not see how the jury can bring in anything but a verdict of Not Guilty."

"I'd like to wring that duck's neck," Freddy said angrily, and Whibley said: "I'll save you the trouble, if I can catch him when Alice and Emma aren't around. Look at 'em, down there in the front row; look at 'em staring at him all starry-eyed, as if he'd just defended 'em from seventeen dragons, instead of having sold 'em out."

CHAPTER

20

The jury wasn't out long. When it had filed back in, Jinx got up. "Your Honor," he said, "we realize that you expect us to give a verdict of Not Guilty."

"That is so," said the judge. "All the evidence we have heard in this case seems to show that the prisoner is innocent."

"Well, we're very sorry," the cat said, "but we think the prisoner ought to go to jail. If he isn't guilty of this crime, he probably is of a lot of others we don't know about. So our verdict is Guilty, and so say we all, and we hope you'll soak him with everything in the book."

Well there was a great uproar at this. There was a lot of cheering and hand-clapping, and there was the wailing and sobbing of the Bismuth family, who were waiting outside the door, and there was the shouting of Mr. Bismuth, protesting that he had been framed, and there was the banging of the judge's gavel which had no effect whatever. But after a while things quieted down. And Judge Willey said:

"The verdict is not in accordance with the evidence, and I must therefore censure you, gentlemen of the jury, very severely." So he gave them a good bawling out. And then he said: "All this that I have said to you has been said in my public capacity, as a judge. Later, in my private capacity, as a private citizen, I shall offer you my warmest congratulations. At that time I shall point out to you that while you were wrong to pronounce him guilty of stealing the jewels, all the evidence in the Wiggins case showed that he was guilty of stealing Miss Mc-Minnickle's purse. So that by sending him to jail, even for the wrong reason, you have done the right thing." He looked at the prisoner with distaste. "I doubt if he could ever go straight, with that nose."

Then the judge got up and had Mr. Bismuth brought before the bench, and sentenced him to two years in jail. And Mr. Bismuth was led away by two large policemen, still shouting his protests.

Freddy, however, was not well satisfied with the result. He said as much to his friend the sheriff, as he was leaving the courtroom. "All that has happened," he said, "is that there's one less Bismuth eating the Beans out of house and home. And you bet Mrs. Bean will be nicer than ever to Mrs. Bismuth and the children, with Mr. Bismuth in jail."

"Well, you ain't done me any favor, Freddy, and that's a fact," the sheriff said gloomily. "We got an awful nice lot of prisoners in my jail this summer. What those boys are going to say when Bismuth turns up! I just hate to face 'em.''

"Hold on!" Freddy said suddenly. "I've got an idea." They were starting down the courthouse steps, then Freddy stopped. "Hold it," he said. "Look."

Ahead of them, Uncle Wesley, followed by his nieces, was starting across the courthouse square to take the road back to the farm. But as he went on, the crowd in the square drew away from them, so that the ducks waddled along in an empty space which opened in front of them and filled in behind them. At first the people just looked, but then someone hissed, and in a minute there were hisses and boos and catcalls, and fists were shaken and a few old vegetables thrown. But through it all Alice and Emma walked on, holding their heads high, while Uncle Wesley slunk along behind, evidently half fainting with shame and fright. But nobody made a move to hit him.

"Oh, well," said Freddy. And he and the sheriff went down to the jail and had a long talk. Whibley was there too, and Jinx. And presently they hammered out a plan.

When Mr. Bismuth was brought down to the jail, the prisoners took one look at him and then gathered to hold an indignation meeting. "Fellow like that," said Looey, "fellow that robs ducks and steals old ladies' pocketbooks when they're passin' him the fruit cake—he ain't any fit companion for self-respecting criminals."

"Ain't it the truth!" said Red Mike. "He's going to give our jail a bad name."

So they sent a committee in to protest to the sheriff.

"Now you boys hold your hosses," the sheriff said. "Freddy here, and 'mongst us, we've got a plan. We've put him in Houdini, and unless somethin' goes awful terrible wrong, he'll be gone for good by morning."

All the cells were named after notorious criminals—Borgia, Jesse James, and so on—and there was great competition among the prisoners to be put in those with the most famous names. Houdini was different, it was named after the famous escape artist. Uncongenial prisoners whom everybody wanted to get rid of were put in Houdini, where the window bars were not cemented in tight, but could just be lifted out

Such prisoners were encouraged to escape, and only very stupid ones managed to spend more than a night or two in Houdini.

So Freddy went home and had a talk with Mrs. Bismuth, and she packed up her stuff in a suitcase and she and the children sneaked quietly down the stairs after Mr. and Mrs. Bean had gone to bed. Uncle Ben was waiting with his old station wagon, and the Bismuths and Jinx and Whibley and Freddy got in, and then Hank and the cows pushed the wagon out of the gate and down the road for a ways before Uncle Ben started the engine. They did this because Uncle Ben had installed a small atomic engine in the wagon, which gave it so much power that when it started it gave several tremendous explosions, and then fairly kicked up its heels before roaring off at terrific speed.

Mr. Bismuth was just dropping off to sleep in his cell that night when a familiar sound roused him. It was his wife crying somewhere, and he thought he could also distinguish the suppressed sniffling and hiccuping of his children as they accompanied her. He sat up. "Ambrosia?" he said in a low voice.

"Oh, children!" Mrs. Bismuth exclaimed.

"It is the voice of your honored pa! Oh, Ed, can you hear me?"

"Of course I can, you idiot!" he replied. "So can everybody else within ten miles. What is it now?"

So Mrs. Bismuth told him that she had got in touch with Uncle Ben, who needed money badly for another trip to Mars, and that he had agreed to rescue Mr. Bismuth and drive him and his family to the bus station, so that they could all go back to Cleveland. All he asked was eighty-three dollars.

"Eighty-three dollars, hey?" said Mr. Bismuth. "Why that's just the amount that I—well, never mind that. You must have beat him down, Ambrosia. 'Tain't very much for rescuin' a Bismuth. Well, you gave him the money, I suppose. You get the rest out from under the floor? —But hold on," he said suddenly. "How'm I to get out? I suppose you didn't think about there being bars on this window!"

So she explained that for an extra fifty dollars, Uncle Ben had arranged to have the sheriff put him in the room with the removable window bars. Mr. Bismuth seemed rather pleased that his escape was costing more than he at first supposed; evidently he had plenty of money. So he took the brace off his nose—he had put it on as usual before going to sleep—and got dressed and climbed out, and Uncle Ben drove them to the bus stop.

So Mrs. Bismuth bought bus tickets to Cleveland. But before the bus came, Mr. Bismuth said suddenly: "Hey, what good is it, our going back to Cleveland? My description will be sent all over the country, and with this nose I'll be recognized within a few days, and the police will grab me and send me back to jail."

"Oh, dear!" said Mrs. Bismuth. "Oh, children, your honored pa is really sunk this time!"

But Old Whibley, who had been hiding in a doorway with Freddy and Jinx, flew out. "I can fix that nose for you," he said. "Police'll never catch you if you have a straight nose," he said, "and I can straighten it. It'll cost you fifty dollars, and it'll hurt. What do you say?"

"Give him the money, Ambrosia," Mr. Bismuth said. "But hold on! You say it'll hurt?"

"Hurt for a minute, or be brought back and stay in jail two years," said the owl. "Well, make up your mind. I hear the bus." And indeed the bus had just turned into the end of the street.

"Well," said Mr. Bismuth. "Well—oh, all right!"

Whibley flew over and perched on his head. He grabbed one ear with one claw and the other ear with the other claw, and then he reached down and took Mr. Bismuth's nose in his powerful beak and gave it a quick hard wrench. Mr. Bismuth let out a yell that brought heads out of windows all down the block, and the bus driver was so startled that he jammed on the brakes and brought the bus to such a sudden stop that all the passengers were thrown violently forward and banged *their* noses on the seats in front of them. And Mrs. Bismuth and the little Bismuths burst into loud yells of "Oh, poor pa!" But Mr. Bismuth's nose was straight. He felt of it, and then he wiped the tears from his eyes and stopped groaning. "Pay him," he said to Mrs. Bismuth. He reached in his pocket and took out his nose brace and threw it into the street, and then he climbed into the bus. And after Whibley had got his fifty dollars, the rest of the Bismuths piled in after him. And the bus drove off in the general direction of Cleveland.

Freddy was pretty pleased. He had got the

eighty-three dollars back for Miss McMinnickle, and he and Whibley between them had collected an extra hundred which would be presented to Mr. Bean, to make up for some of the damage and expense they had suffered. In addition, Mrs. Bismuth had packed a large sack with canned goods which she had taken from Mrs. Bean's shelves, but she had forgotten it, and it was still in the station wagon. Freddy and Jinx sang all the way home, and Uncle Ben grunted along tunelessly with them, and even Old Whibley provided a deep Oompah, oom-pah accompaniment.

"Oh, how beautiful seems the scenery
As we return to a happy Beanery," Jinx sang.
"We're going to visit all the planets
So wash your shirt and press your panits,"
 Freddy replied.

For he now had begun to work on an idea which became later so profitable to him: the space cruises in Uncle Ben's rocket, organized under the name of Bean, Peppercorn, Bean and Bean. Which is to say Benjamin Bean, Mrs. Peppercorn, William F. Bean and Frederick Bean.

Freddy and Jinx sang all the way home.

When they reached the farm, Uncle Ben drove into the barnyard and stopped the car. As they got out, Freddy looked up into the sky, which was glittering with stars. "Well, there she is," he said. "There's New Beanland."

"Sure of that?" Old Whibley asked. "Sure it isn't the earth, and this isn't the planet you were aiming at?"

Uncle Ben shook his head. "Ain't sure yet," he said. "Might be the same."

"That's just it," said the owl. "Mars and the earth might be just the same—same seas and continents, same trees and animals, exactly the same people. You'll never know, pig. And that's a thought for you to sleep on." He spread his wings and drifted off into the night.

"Well," said Jinx, "whether the earth, or whether New Beania
I'm awful glad I've been and seen ya."

"Maybe I'm really on Mars after all," Freddy thought. "Maybe Whibley's right, and we got there and don't know it." This speculation worried him; after he got into his comfortable bed in the pig pen it kept him awake for nearly five minutes.

A NOTE ON THE TYPE

The text of this book was set on the Linotype in Baskerville. Linotype Baskerville is a facsimile cutting from type cast from the original matrices of a face designed by John Baskerville. The original face was the forerunner of the "modern" group of type faces.

John Baskerville (1706-75), of Birmingham, England, a writing-master, with a special renown for cutting inscriptions in stone, began experimenting about 1750 with punch-cutting and making typographical material. It was not until 1757 that he published his first work. His types, at first criticized, in time were recognized as both distinct and elegant, and his types as well as his printing were greatly admired.

Composed, printed, and bound by H. Wolff, New York

Freddy Books Published By
The Overlook Press

FREDDY THE DETECTIVE
by Walter R. Brooks
ISBN 978-1-59020-418-4 • $9.99 • PB

Freddy is inspired while reading *The Adventures of Sherlock Holmes* to become a detective. Setting out with his intrepid partner Mrs. Wiggins the cow, he is ultimately challenged to prove that Jinx the cat was framed for murder.

FREDDY THE POLITICIAN
by Walter R. Brooks
ISBN 978-1-59020-419-1 • $9.99 • PB

Freddy, the good-natured pig with a poetic soul, is promoting a campaign to get Mrs. Wiggins, the cow, elected president of the First Animal Republic. As he himself is an officer in the newly organized First Animal Bank, he has more than a modicum of influence—if he can just figure out how to use it.

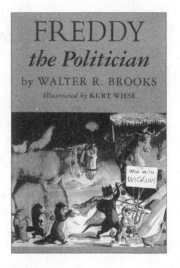

THE OVERLOOK PRESS
New York
www.overlookpress.com

Freddy Books Published By
The Overlook Press

FREDDY AND THE BEAN HOME NEWS
by Walter R. Brooks
ISBN 978-1-59020-420-7 · $9.99 · PB

When Freddy's friend Mr. Dimsey is ousted for publishing news of Bean Farm in the local newspaper, the animals decide to take action and publish the first animal newspaper *The Bean Home News*—with Freddy as editor-in-chief, of course! But everyone's favorite pig discovers that being a newspaperman isn't as easy as it looks!

FREDDY AND THE POPINJAY
by Walter R. Brooks
ISBN 978-1-59020-469-6 · $9.99 · PB

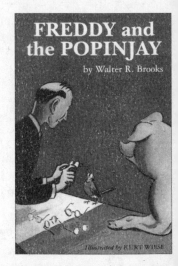

A robin with poor eyesight has mistaken Freddy the pig's tail for a worm. Putting aside the poem he is writing, Freddy decides to help the poor bird solve his problem. But the solution just seems to lead to bigger problems.

THE OVERLOOK PRESS
New York
www.overlookpress.com